The Case of the Missing Coffee Pot

The Case of the Missing Coffee Pot

From the Case Files of Attorney Daniel Marcos

Jeffery Sealing

iUniverse LLC
Bloomington

The Case of the Missing Coffee Pot
From the Case Files of Attorney Daniel Marcos

This fictional case is based on Colorado Revised Statutes. Therefore, Colorado Law Procedures, Title 16 and the Criminal Code, Title 18 are mentioned or referenced for legal definitions only. Always consult an attorney in all legal cases. The town named is real but no longer exists. The town, for the purposes of this book, was placed outside of Silverton, Colorado for security reasons due to the September 11, 2001 terrorist attacks. Other towns mentioned are real as they are in the counties mentioned.

iUniverse books may be ordered through booksellers or by contacting:

iUniverse LLC
1663 Liberty Drive
Bloomington, IN 47403
www.iuniverse.com
1-800-Authors (1-800-288-4677)

ISBN: 978-1-4917-1504-8 (sc)
ISBN: 978-1-4917-1505-5 (e)

Printed in the United States of America.

iUniverse rev. date: 11/20/2013

Even the mundane in our lives can sometimes hide the most spectacular. Don't discount a small detail. Jeffery Sealing

To Karena and Bill at the Blue Moon Akita Rescue in Denver, Colorado for letting us adopt Ricky. Ricky is a rescue Akita; check them out at www.bluemoonakitarescue.com.

CHAPTER 1

The first rays of dawn were striking the fourteeners around Ironton and Silverton, Colorado. Daniel was just getting out of surgery and being placed into a private room in the ICU ward. There were also extra security and police personnel outside the room and in the waiting area as well as on patrol in the parking lots and surrounding areas to the hospital.

The chief trauma surgeon had just gotten off the phone with Marshal Beckman and was putting Daniel into a medically induced coma. This was so that Daniel's body could get all the uninterrupted sleep it needed. Jill was pulling up to the Ironton Town Marshal's office and getting out of her vehicle with her copy of the local newspaper which she hadn't had a chance to read yet.

Jill walked up the steps towards the office when she saw Daniel's SUV in the impound lot behind the office. It was badly damaged with body damage on all four doors, bloodstains on what was left of the front windshield and one flat, passenger side front tire. She still wasn't feeling much better from whatever had made her sick the night before, but she knew she had to relieve Jason.

Jill passed Mary, one of the reporters/photographers from the local newspaper, as she entered the office. Jason looked up with red, tear-filled eyes as he handed each of the drunk and disorderlies, from last night, their court summons. Jill looked at Jason rather strangely.

"Long night, Jason?" asked Jill, smiling and pouring herself a cup of coffee. She then sat down at her desk.

"Yes, Jill, a very long night," replied Jason hoarsely.

"Is that Daniel Marcos' SUV in our impound lot?"

"Yes," replied Jason, flatly grabbing the CD that Mary had just dropped off for him.

"Did he have an accident or did you arrest him for a DUI?" asked Jill as she started to open up the newspaper she had been carrying.

"No, he was assaulted by four people last night. Jill, when you take over my job in a few years when I retire, there will be a couple of times in your career that you will feel useless as a police officer."

Jill had just read the newspaper's front-page headline: LOCAL ATTORNEY ASSAULTED.

"Like last night?" said Jill reading the article.

"Yes and this is the fourth time in my twenty plus year career in law enforcement that I couldn't help someone. I could hear everything, but I couldn't do anything," he said as he grabbed the CD that was coming out of his computer.

The door opened to the office and in walked the reverend for the local church and Nancy, the Silverton Town Marshal. Jason took the CD and put it into the same left, front jacket pocket that Mary's CD had been put into a few minutes earlier. He turned to face Jill.

"We will be back in a few minutes, Jill. If you need me, get me on the radio," said Jason, pointing to the portable radio handset that was attached to the left side of his jacket.

"Yes, Jason," she replied as they left the office.

Jason, Nancy and the reverend started walking down the street towards Daniel's office. They all walked into Daniel's outer office and stood facing Lynn. A few seconds later, Jessica Kim entered the office. Jessica saw the reverend, Jason and Nancy and figured that Daniel must have been arrested for something terrible. Lynn spoke first.

"I'm sorry, Marshal Beckman, but Daniel's not here. I've been trying to reach him all morning," said Lynn.

"I have some rather bad news about Daniel," said Jason, solemnly.

2

Jason told both Lynn and Jessica what was going on with Daniel. When Jason had finished, he took out the CD's he had brought with him. Tears were filling up everyone's eyes as Jason pulled out his field notebook to ask a few questions that he had written down earlier in the morning.

"First, let me tell you something, Lynn and Jessica. Daniel and I have had our differences in the past, but he is a professional. Nobody had the right to do this to him. I will do my best to bring to justice those responsible for this attack," said Jason as his voice started to crack.

"Lynn, Jessica, I arrested the only person who was at the scene. He isn't saying much. But, I want to show you his mug shot and see if either of you recognize him," said Nancy as she handed the photo to each of them. Although Jessica didn't recognize him, Lynn did.

"Nancy, that man was in this office a few days ago. He said something to Daniel about not sticking his nose in where it didn't belong," she said as she almost cried.

"Calm down, Lynn," said Nancy.

"Or words to that effect?" asked Jason as he started writing in his field notebook again.

"Yes."

"Lynn and Jessica, I want you both to look over the pictures on those CD's I'm going to give you. Tell me, at your earliest convenience, if anything in those photos I took of Daniel's SUV is missing or if there is anything extra," said Jason handing Lynn the CD's.

"Okay, Jason," she said, taking the CD's and putting them into her top desk drawer.

"The doctors at the hospital need to know if Daniel has either a Living Will or a Durable Medical Power of Attorney and who is responsible for those documents," said Jason.

"Daniel has both, or so he told me when I was hired. Since the previous secretary died in a skiing accident, I will assume that the duties fall upon me," said Lynn, almost crying once again.

"Lynn, relax, you're doing fine. You and Jessica are the only official visitors that Daniel is allowed to have. He is being heavily guarded until he leaves the hospital," said Jason.

"Which hospital in Durango is he at?" asked Jessica, trying not to cry.

"He was airlifted to St. Mary-Corwin in Grand Junction," said Nancy.

"Now, I will pass along this information to the doctors in Grand Junction. If you don't have any questions for me, I will leave now," said Jason as he left.

"Lynn, the doctors may need copies of the paperwork sent to them," said Nancy.

The door to the office opened and in walked Sherrie and Aaron. Aaron started looking around the office and saw a picture of Daniel. Daniel was in his workout attire and Aaron smiled. Sherrie and Aaron sat down and waited for Nancy to leave. The reverend stood up and handed both Jessica and Lynn his business card.

"I am so sorry, Lynn and Jessica. This is a very difficult time for the both of you. My twenty-four hour number is on the back; don't hesitate to call me anytime," he said.

"Thank you, reverend. I thought you might harbor some ill will towards him because he is a lawyer," said Lynn taking the card.

"Yes, he is a lawyer, but I echo Marshal Beckman's compliment. Daniel is a professional in the times that I have seen him in court with his clients. Everyone in the court room responds to him and he is never condescending even if you make a mistake."

"Thank you again, reverend. Do you have any suggestions for this crisis?" asked Jessica.

"Maintain your daily rituals, exercise is important and keep Daniel in your thoughts and prayers; goodbye," said the reverend as he prepared to leave.

The reverend left as Lynn stood up to greet the potential new clients. Sherrie stood up and shook Lynn's extended left hand. Aaron stood up as well and they both approached Lynn's desk. Aaron looked Jessica up and down once. He took in her beautiful Asian female qualities, and then he returned his attention to Sherrie.

"Can I help you two?" asked Lynn, trying not to cry.

"Yes, my name is Sherrie Zappatta and this is Aaron. We are here to pick up Bob Quinest's personal effects," she said.

"Oh, yes, let me pull the file on this case," said Lynn as she turned to face the three drawer filing cabinet that was to the left of her desk. She pulled the file out and handed it to Sherrie.

Sherrie looked over all the paperwork. Everything seemed in perfect order until she reached the Lien on the Estate of Bob Quinest paperwork. She looked it over and closed the file folder back up, sticking it underneath her right arm.

"How much is that lien for?"

"$3,881.80 for medical bills, ambulance trip, doctor's fees and replacement of damaged personal and business property."

"Do you take plastic?" asked Sherrie as she pulled out the company business card.

"Sure do," replied Lynn as she ran the credit card through the scanner. She had Sherrie sign the top slip, while Lynn retained the bottom slip. Lynn then handed Sherrie back the credit card.

"Sherrie, could I please get a business card from you as well as a copy of your attorney credentials or a driver's license for the file?" asked Lynn.

"Sure," replied Sherrie as she fumbled around in her purse for her attorney's credentials. She handed them to Lynn, who made copies and handed them back to Sherrie.

"May I go now?" asked Sherrie.

"Yes, you may go and thank you," said Lynn as she went back to doing some paperwork.

As they left, Aaron stopped at the door and turned to face Lynn.

"You're one lucky secretary, Miss Lyons; Mr. Marcos is one very attractive man," he said as he let the door close behind himself.

Lynn and Jessica were alone now in the office. They looked at each other for several minutes, before they broke down and cried. Lynn put a tissue box on her desk so that they could share it. Lynn blew her nose and spoke to Jessica.

"What were you trying to tell me before we were interrupted?" asked Lynn.

"I have my report here for Daniel; no rush. I'll have the photos I took at the facility ready next week," said Jessica, handing Lynn the report.

"Thank you; anything else?" asked Lynn, taking the report.

"Tell Daniel, again, no hurry, that the infrared photos I took at the facility will be developed and sent back to me. I have receipts for sending and returning the photos via mail," said Jessica, handing Lynn the various receipts.

"Great, I'll put them in the file folder. Did the photo lab say how long before you would be getting those photos back?"

"About ten to fourteen weeks."

"Why so long?"

"The only lab in the U.S. that can develop that infrared film is in New Jersey."

"I understand now. Let's start looking at those pictures," said Lynn putting the CD's into her computer.

As they looked over the pictures, both of them made notes. When they finished off the pictures, they went their separate ways. Lynn went to the bank to get into the safe deposit boxes as Jessica went back to her office to type up some reports. As Lynn walked up to the Teller Supervisor, Melanie Thompson, Melanie smiled at Lynn.

"Hello, Lynn, we all read about what happened to Daniel. We're really sorry. If there is anything we can do, as the bank, to help, let us know," said Melanie.

"Thank you, Melanie. I need to get into the business safe deposit box and possibly Daniel's personal safe deposit box," said Lynn, fumbling around inside of her purse with her right hand looking for the keys.

"Sure; Amy, could you handle customers while I go back into the safe deposit box room with Miss Lyons, here?" asked Melanie.

"Be glad to watch the counter," said Amy.

Melanie let Lynn into the safe deposit box room inside of the outer vault. Lynn opened the business safe deposit box first. Melanie showed Lynn into a privacy room so she could go through the contents. Lynn found Daniel's living will, durable medical power of attorney, a general power of attorney and a special power of attorney for Lynn. She took the documents out of the safe deposit box and opened the door to the room. Melanie was just finishing up helping out a customer when she turned around to face Lynn.

"Are you done, Lynn?" asked Melanie closing her cash drawer and locking it up. She then took her keys with her.

"Not exactly, can you make copies of these documents?" asked Lynn as she choked on her words.

"Sure," said Melanie as she took the documents and returned a short time later from the back of the vault.

Melanie handed the copies and the originals back to Lynn. Lynn went back into the privacy room and emerged a few minutes later. After the safe deposit box was secured back inside the vault, Lynn left the bank with her copies. She walked down the street to the marshal's office and entered. Jason and Jill both looked up.

"How are you, Lynn?" asked Jason.

"As good as can be expected. I've had a chance to go over those pictures on the CD's you gave me. Do you want those CD's back?" asked Lynn as she pulled out a piece of paper that Jessica had given her to give to Jason or Jill before she left the office.

"No, you can destroy them. Did you find something?" asked Jason as he pulled out his field notebook and attached pen to take notes.

"I think so; I assume that you have Daniel's large briefcase, cell phone and his weapon, right?"

"I don't have his weapon, and I do not have the large briefcase; only the small one that I found at the scene and no I don't have his cell phone either. I assumed I would find it at the crime scene, and I didn't."

"Jason, Daniel always kept his large briefcase in the backseat of his SUV."

"Okay, don't panic yet. Were there any items of value in the large briefcase?"

"Yes, there would have been about a hundred dollars in cash, his cell phone and two, British Commando knives. The briefcase may have had his Glock® Model 20, several magazines and client notes."

"Have you checked the office or his home for those items, yet?"

"No, not yet."

"Okay, take your time and search for them. If you don't find them, call my office immediately; is there anything else?"

"I have a piece of paper here for you from Jessica is all," she said, handing Jason the paper.

Lynn returned to the office to find Linda waiting for her. Lynn opened the door and they walked into the office together. Linda waited to speak to Lynn until she had sat down at her desk. Lynn pulled out the CD's from her computer. She then turned around behind her desk and turned on the shredder. She destroyed the CD's, turned off the shredder and faced Linda.

"Sorry to keep you waiting, what can I do for you, Linda?"

"I don't like Daniel very much, mostly because he shows me where I make all of my mistakes. But, Daniel is a professional to everyone including me. Whoever did this to him, I will fully prosecute."

"Thank you, Linda. What about the guy that Nancy is holding?"

"He's been charged with being an accessory to the fact, Colorado Revised Statutes 18-8-105, of First Degree Assault, Colorado Revised Statutes 18-3-202. If Daniel should die, the charge will be moved up to Second Degree Murder, Colorado Revised Statutes 18-3-103. Either way, he's looking at a lengthy sentence."

"That's very kind of you, Linda."

"I will surmise that Daniel would want the accused moved up here to Silverton. I already made the arrangements."

"Thank you again, Linda. I will get that request over to your office as soon as I can."

"Take your time."

"Linda, Daniel was subpoenaed to be in court Thursday morning for the Hawthorne case and to give a statement in Durango at your satellite office. Also, I believe that Mr. Berman is scheduled for his arraignment in the morning as well."

"I will release Daniel from those subpoenas. I have the police officer's report and the evidence from the flash drive. That will be sufficient for a conviction."

"What about the statement? Will you, or your satellite office, accept a signed, notarized copy of his statement?" asked Lynn as she pulled out the copy from a pending file on her desktop.

"I will accept the notarized copy on Daniel's behalf."

"Here it is," said Lynn, handing her the statement.

"Thank you, Lynn. I'll see you and the accused in court tomorrow morning," she said as she left the office.

Jessica entered the office a short time later.

CHAPTER 2

Jessica and Lynn went to lunch. Jessica was all excited about a letter and a large package that had arrived. As they ate their lunch, Jessica talked about her special school she was going to attend in three weeks.

"Daniel's letter of recommendation got me into the school. Normally, the school doesn't let non-law enforcement personnel into the classes that I will be taking, but Daniel's letter did it," she said.

"That's great news. How long are you going to be gone?"

"About five weeks. I received the package and letter today at the same time."

"When are you planning on leaving?"

"Next Friday."

"Could I borrow your four-wheel drive to go see Daniel?"

"Better yet, I'll go with you."

"Thanks."

Their lunch arrived and they ate in silence. They walked up to the register to pay when the café's owner stepped out from behind a stove.

"Lynn and Jessica, until this crisis with Daniel is over, feel free to have breakfast, lunch and dinner here; I'll pick up the tab," he said.

"Thank you, but Daniel would want me to pay you something," said Lynn.

"Well, we will discuss the matter when Daniel feels better."

Lynn and Jessica left the café and went their separate ways once again. Lynn received the mail when it was delivered. She began to thoroughly search the office for some of the missing items. She found Daniel's Glock® Model 20 in the top, right desk drawer. Lynn immediately called Marshal Beckman with the news she had found the gun. However, she still had not found the cell phone.

Marshal Beckman asked Lynn for the cell phone number. Lynn continued taking care of business until closing time. She made one last phone call to retired Judge Dale Lutezenberg as was Daniel's wish on the special power of attorney paperwork. Dale wasn't in, so Lynn left him a message, locked up the office and went home.

The next morning, Lynn arrived at work early as usual. She unlocked the door, disarmed the alarm system and made some coffee. She then locked the main doors back up until 8:00 a.m. Lynn unlocked the door and sat back down at her desk. She started doing paperwork and other duties, when an elderly gentleman walked into the office. Lynn recognized the man as retired Judge Lutezenberg. He smiled and shook Lynn's outstretched, right hand.

"I got your message last night. Can you fill me in on the way to the courthouse?" he asked in a pleasant tone of voice, while drooling on himself.

"Sure," replied Lynn, handing Dale a tissue to wipe off the drool.

On the way to the courthouse, Lynn filled Dale in on what was going on. They walked into Judge Larry Bishop's courtroom. Bill was already seated at the defendant's table. Lynn sat down at the table along with Dale. Dale looked over at Linda who smiled at Dale. Dale nodded his head up and down. The Bailiff walked over to the defendant's table.

"It is good to see you, Your Honor Lutezenberg," said Sergio shaking Dale's left hand as Dale looked somewhat past the Bailiff.

"Thank you, Mr. Martinez; it is good to see you."

The Bailiff returned to his post in the far left corner of the courtroom. Dale turned to Lynn.

"What is Daniel's normal protocol?"

"At the arraignment, he waives the reading of the charges, informs the judge that the accused has been advised of his Constitutional rights, pleads not guilty on behalf of the client and requests to go to the preliminary hearing as soon as possible to discuss reasonable bail."

"He follows the script that I wrote for him so many years ago."

The door at the left of the courtroom opened. Sergio stood up to address the courtroom. Dale started to drool on himself again; Lynn saw this and grabbed some tissue from a tissue box that was located on the right side of the defendant's table. She gave the tissue to Dale to wipe off the drool. Judge Larry Bishop had entered the courtroom.

"All rise, criminal court for the 6th Judicial District in the town of Silverton in the county of San Juan is now in session. The Honorable Judge Larry Bishop, presiding," said Sergio.

Larry had walked up the three steps to his bench and sat down. He put on his reading glasses and opened the case file. Everyone remained standing until Larry spoke.

"You may be seated. These court proceedings are going to be recorded by my court clerk electronically. Does either defense or prosecution have a problem with this for any reason?" he asked.

"None, Your Honor," said Linda.

"None, Your Honor," said Dale as he started to drool on himself again.

"So noted, this is the arraignment hearing in the case of *The People v. Bill Berman,* 14CR299. Is the defendant present?" asked Larry.

"I am, Your Honor," said Bill standing up and then sitting back down.

"So noted, is the defendant represented by any legal counsel?"

"He is, Your Honor. Dale Lutezenberg, retired judge, former prosecutor and criminal defense attorney," said Dale as he looked to the far left of Larry, almost out the windows that were to Dale's left.

"Your Honor Lutezenberg, didn't you have a stroke in open court a few years ago?" asked Larry.

"I did, Your Honor. I was officially medically retired from the bench. However, my attorney credentials are still active and valid until March of 2015; I have them present for you to check," said Dale as he pulled out his ID wallet from his left, back pocket. He then dropped this ID onto the desktop.

"Bailiff, would you please bring me the ID?" asked Larry.

"Yes, Your Honor."

Sergio walked over to the table, picked up the ID and handed it to Larry. Larry looked it over and was satisfied that Dale was telling the truth. He handed the ID back to Sergio who walked it back to Dale. Dale put his ID back into his back, left pocket.

"Is the State ready?"

"We are, Your Honor. We have some concerns over the accused's legal counsel; specifically, his competency," said Linda, looking at Dale while he started drooling.

"So noted. Your Honor Lutezenberg, what is your current physical and mental status?" asked Larry.

"I am as physically and mentally fit as I can be for someone my age, sixty, who has had a stroke. I cannot see out of my left eye, without a very hideous helmet looking device to wear and I have a tendency to drool out of the left side of my mouth," he said spitting onto the desktop.

"Drooling, like what you're doing right now, Your Honor?" asked Larry.

Lynn quickly passed some more tissues to Dale. Dale wiped off the drool that was running down his chin and threw the used tissue into the trash can that was to the left of the table.

"Yes, Your Honor, just like that. I believe that, so long as I have a sufficient supply of tissue and a place to put the used tissue, I can sufficiently defend the client," replied Dale as he sat down.

"So noted. Bailiff, if His Honor is in my courtroom again, please make sure that there is an ample supply of tissue boxes placed on the defendant's table," said Larry.

"I will make sure that there is an ample supply of tissue boxes and trash cans to put the used tissues into, Your Honor," said Sergio.

"Objection, Your Honor. I believe the State would like to know and has a right to know how His Honor here was made defense counsel for the accused?" asked Linda.

"Objection noted; defense counsel, will you answer the question?" asked Larry.

"I certainly can, Your Honor. Daniel left a general power of attorney allowing His Honor here to dispose of any of Daniel's pending cases. Daniel also left a special power of attorney allowing me to sign for His Honor, due to his left side disability. His Honor normally would sign with his left hand, but since he cannot use it, I will be able to sign for him," said Lynn handing Linda a copy of the documents.

"Does the State have any problems with the documents or explanation given by defense counsel?" asked Larry.

"None, Your Honor," replied Linda, taking the paperwork.

"So noted. I surmise that the State is ready with sufficient evidence to prosecute the accused?"

"The State is ready," said Linda.

"So noted. Is defense counsel ready with a plea and do you wish to make any statements to this court?"

"The defense is ready. My client pleads not guilty to the charges being levied against him by the State. My client has been advised of his Constitutional rights by myself, law enforcement personnel and Daniel. My client waives a reading of the charges," said Dale as he passed some tissue by Lynn for his drool. Larry was watching this intently.

Dale wiped off his chin and looked past Larry as he collected his thoughts again. Larry looked at Dale with some concern in his mind.

"Are you done, defense counsel?" asked Larry.

"With drooling? Yes, Your Honor. My client requests to set the preliminary hearing as soon as possible to discuss reasonable bail."

"So noted. Does the State object to defense counsel's request?"

"No objections, Your Honor," said Linda.

"So noted. Let me look at my court docket so see when I have an available time," said Larry as he reviewed his court docket. He found next Thursday was open.

"Does next Thursday, the 18th, sound acceptable to both parties?"

"Agreed, Your Honor," said Dale.

"No objections, Your Honor," said Linda.

"So noted. This arraignment hearing is over. The accused is hereby remanded back into the custody of the Silverton Town Marshal," said Larry, banging down his gavel.

"All rise," said Sergio as Larry left his courtroom.

Melanie Thompson had been watching the whole courtroom scene with her oldest son. She left with him, sent him back to school and waited outside the courthouse for Lynn to emerge. Dale and Lynn walked out of the courthouse where they ran into Melanie. Dale was wiping drool off of his chin and Lynn was opening the passenger-side, front door for Dale. Melanie approached Lynn cautiously.

"Lynn, do you have time to answer a minor legal question?" asked Melanie.

"Sure," said Lynn as she shut the door.

"Can my employer force me to take a polygraph test?" she asked, nervously.

"Certain employers can. Since I don't have my notes on the Employee Polygraph Protection Act of 1988 as Amended in 2010, I can't go into specifics."

"I kind of thought you might not go into details, here."

"Is your employer planning on giving you or forcing you to take a polygraph test?"

"Yes, that's the rumor going around work right now."

"Stop by the office by 5:00 p.m. and we will talk."

"Okay."

Lynn stepped into her car and drove back to the office. She went about taking care of paperwork, while Dale went into Daniel's inner office to go through the evidence that had been delivered. Dale sat down at Daniel's desk. He picked up Daniel's legal pad that had all sorts of notes on it. Dale couldn't make much out of the notes, so he waited until Lynn had started a pot of coffee before he said anything to her.

"Lynn, since you probably know more about how Daniel thinks, you're going to have to help me sort through his notes," said Dale, drooling.

"Yes, Your Honor, I will assist you as best I can. Here's some tissue," she said handing him some tissue to wipe off the drool.

15

"As far as taking your LSAT exam tomorrow, go ahead and take it. Daniel already approved the time off and he would want you to take the test. It is a very important test for you. If you need a reference for anything, just give them my name and number."

"Thank you, Your Honor, but I'm not really sure that I want to take that test right now," she said.

"Take the test and then go see Daniel. Does Daniel have a private investigator he uses?"

"Yes, her name is Jessica Kim."

"Please have her come to the office after lunch. I'm hungry, let's go eat," said Dale wiping drool off of his chin and following Lynn out the door.

They went and ate at the local café. When they returned, Dale started going through the boxes of evidence. He was drinking a cup of coffee with cream and sugar in it, while reviewing the video and audio surveillance evidence, when Melanie entered the outer office. Melanie sat down to the left of Lynn's desk.

"According to the EPPA law of 1988 as Amended in 2010, if you work around money or anything of high value, or if you work as an armored car driver, ATM technician etc., your employer has the right to give you a polygraph or lie detector test at any time during your employment. You can refuse it, but that wouldn't look very good," said Lynn.

"I kind of figured that, can I have an attorney present during the test?"

"You can, if you want, it is your 5th and 6th Amendment rights that will be protected if you decide to have an attorney present with you. Is there something going on at work?"

"Yes, the rumor is that someone at the bank stole one hundred thousand dollars over a five-year period of time."

"And that person is you, right?"

"Yes. Lynn, I didn't do it, but I strongly suspect whoever did steal the money is trying to blame me for it, but good."

"Has anyone questioned you about the theft?"

"Yes, so far only the insurance company investigator. His name is Kyle Coats; he seems to be a real nice man."

"Is he from the FDIC?"

"No, the bank is small enough that the FDIC won't insure us. We have to pay a fee to a private insurance company that insures the funds in the bank to the FDIC limits."

"This insurance policy is FDIC type, then?" asked Lynn as she had already started taking notes.

"Yes."

"What exactly do you do for the bank?"

"I'm the Teller Supervisor. I've been with the Ironton Town Bank and Trust for seven years. I'm a divorced mother of three boys and I don't want to go to prison for something I didn't do."

"I understand, Melanie. Theft in that amount of money is life in prison without parole."

"That's what the insurance investigator told me, too. Should I take the polygraph test?"

Dale had heard part of the conversation and appeared in the outer office doorway. He was drooling again.

"Absolutely not, madam, if your employer tries to order you to take the polygraph, or lie detector, test, you tell them no. Then you invoke your 5th Amendment right to remain silent and send your employer to come see me."

"Thank you, sir."

"Anytime, madam; Lynn, when Jessica gets here, I'll need you both to come into the office. Bring a notepad and some motions paperwork."

"Yes, Your Honor. Have a good day, Melanie."

"Thank you," she said as she left the office.

Jessica showed up right after Lynn had put the receiver of the phone down into its cradle. Dale had Lynn lock the outer doors so that they could start going through the evidence very thoroughly. Shortly after a late dinner, Dale had Lynn drive him back home. He told Jessica that he would meet her at the office in the morning. On the trip home, Lynn asked Dale how he had arrived at the office earlier in the day. Dale told her that Jill Halverston had given him a ride.

Melanie arrived at home to find a strange man waiting for her in the driveway. The man approached her and showed her his law enforcement credentials. He then spoke to her calmly.

17

"Mrs. Melanie Thompson, I'm Special Agent Larry Homes of the FBI. I want to talk to you," he said.

"Won't you come inside, Mr. Homes?" asked Melanie as she opened the door and shut it quickly.

CHAPTER 3

Jessica assisted Dale into the office, started a pot of coffee and checked the phone messages. Dale started going through the evidence once again. Jessica came into Daniel's inner office with a cup of coffee for Dale and herself. She set his cup of coffee down to his right side along with some creamer and sugar. He looked down at Daniel's notepad to try and make some sense of Daniel's notes. Dale wiped some drool off of his chin.

"Miss Kim, would you mind taking some notes and leaving them for Lynn on Monday morning?" asked Dale, nicely.

"Not a problem," she replied, grabbing a legal pad from Lynn's desktop, along with a pen.

"First, have Lynn file a Motion to Suppress Evidence that is contained in evidence boxes one through four. It is the evidence that was used at the federal level case and it doesn't apply to this case," he said, drooling. Jessica handed him a tissue.

"Anything else, Your Honor?" asked Jessica as she wrote down the note.

"Yes, Miss Kim, could you move a little further to your left, please? I'm almost totally blind in my left eye without a hideous head contraption to allow me to see out of it."

"Yes, Your Honor," said Jessica as she moved over one chair to her left.

"Thank you; now, take a look at this video from about an hour or so before the shooting. What do you think that black thing is that the camera followed?" he asked as he pushed the PLAY button on the DVD player.

Jessica watched the video and then Dale pushed the STOP button when the black thing disappeared into some trashcans. Dale spoke to her after a few minutes.

"What do you think that thing is?" asked Dale.

"First thought is it's an animal, but it could be a person," she replied, handing Dale some tissue.

"A possibility, Miss Kim. Find out from the Colorado Division of Wildlife what animals are dark colored and active at this altitude," he said, wiping drool off of his chin.

"Will do. What if it turns out to be a person?"

"How do we, as the defense, prove that it is a person? As a former prosecutor, I could claim it was an animal. By the same token, how can we prove, to the jury, that the black object is a person?"

Jessica was quiet for a few minutes before she spoke.

"Find out the distance the camera is from the trashcans and the possibility that the person touched them means fingerprints."

"Very good, Miss Kim; make some phone calls now while I look over more of Daniel's notes."

As Dale reviewed more of Daniel's notes and wiped drool off of his chin, Jessica made some phone calls. She put a call into Barry, but since Barry was already doing something else, he said he would call her back. She handled a couple of other phone calls when Barry called back. Jessica took down all the information and returned to the inner office.

"What did you find out?" asked Dale, wiping drool off of his chin.

"The Colorado Division of Wildlife officer I talked to says bear, wolverine and elk are dark in color, but only elk are active year round. Bears are not active at this altitude until late May. The wolverine is in this state, but is rarely seen."

"Good work, Miss Kim. Now I can prove to the prosecution, the judge and the jury that the black object in the surveillance video is more than likely a person. Daniel's notes on this case seem to indicate he thinks that person is one Bob Quinest."

"That would seem about right," mumbled Jessica under her breath.

"What did you find out about the camera?" asked Dale as he began to drool again. Jessica handed him some tissue.

"The distance to the trashcans, Barry estimated, is about 30-yards/10-meters."

"All right, that lends more credibility to the object being a person more than an animal. Do we, as the defense, know if the date and time stamp on the video surveillance is accurate?"

"According to Barry, the camera number, in this case number twenty-nine and the date and time stamp are accurate."

"How accurate?"

Jessica started looking over her notes that she had taken earlier.

"The surveillance camera system at that particular facility uses the date and time from the atomic clock which is located in Connecticut."

"So we, as the defense, will surmise that the atomic clock takes into account the time differential between Eastern Standard Time and Mountain Standard Time along with Daylight Saving Time."

Before Jessica could answer, the office door opened. Jessica walked out front to see who it was. Melanie Thompson walked up to Lynn's desk. Jessica shook Melanie's right hand as Dale walked out into the outer office to get another cup of coffee. As he stirred his sugar and coffee creamer into his coffee, he eavesdropped on the conversation.

"Would you let Lynn know that the FBI came and talked to me last night," said Melanie.

"Will do," replied Jessica as she wrote down the message for Lynn to review later.

Dale turned around to face Melanie.

"Did the FBI search your home?" asked Dale as he began drooling.

"Yes, Your Honor, he did," replied Melanie, trying to keep a straight face while watching the drool run down his chin.

"Did this FBI agent have a search warrant?"

"No, I gave them permission to search my home."

"A permissive search is okay. Did you tell him where he could not search?"

"Yes, I told him to stay out of my kids' rooms."

"Did they search those areas?"

"No, he left after he had searched all the other places in my home."

"They could be getting a search warrant. Heard anymore about the lie detector test?"

"Nothing new, Your Honor. I plan on refusing it anyway and sending them to see you."

"We will be expecting them."

"Have a good day, Your Honor and thank you for your advice."

"You won't be thanking me when I send you my bill," said Dale, smiling and drooling as Melanie left the office.

Jessica waited a few minutes before speaking as they walked into Daniel's inner office.

"I would never have let law enforcement search anything of mine without a search warrant," she said handing Dale some tissue.

"Miss Kim, there are three exceptions to search warrants that a court of law will recognize as legitimate. Therefore, any evidence gained from those types of searches is admissible in court."

"And what are those exceptions?"

"The inevitable discovery Doctrine from a famous U.S. Supreme Court case officially called *Nix v. Williams,* 461 U.S. 437. It is also known as the Christian Burial Speech."

He paused to wipe drool off of his chin again.

"The Verbal Permissive search, which our client used and the Inventory of alleged abandoned personal effects, such as a dead person's personal effects, allegedly abandoned motor vehicles, etc."

"Then the evidence gathered would be admissible in court?"

"Yes, but if during the Permissive Search, law enforcement personnel search an area, place or thing that the property owner or property controller says not to search, then that evidence would be inadmissible."

Jessica looked a little confused, so Dale wiped drool off of his chin again and explained the principle to her.

"Miss Kim, let's say you get pulled over and Marshal Beckman wants to search your car. You can say yes, but you can say, don't search the glove box, trunk or gym bag, etc. If Marshal Beckman searches any of those off limits areas you said not to search, the evidence gathered during that search would be inadmissible in court."

"You speak as if that statement was from experience," she said, smiling.

"It did come from a case many years ago. The police officers and the court were very embarrassed, to say the least."

Both of them started laughing as they went back to going through the other evidence in the case. Dale went over more of Daniel's notes and then set down the notepad before lunchtime. After lunch, they returned to the office. Jessica accepted the mail and found that Barry had called. She called Barry back as Dale picked up the notepad once again. Jessica took quick notes during their conversation before going into Daniel's inner office. Dale looked up and smiled, drooling. Jessica handed him some tissue.

"Thank you, now I understand from Lynn that you are going to a very special school, is that right?" asked Dale.

"Yes, a letter Daniel wrote swayed the trainer to let me attend the school. I'll be gone for about five weeks."

"What school are you going to attend?"

"John Hopkins University has a course for their CVSA software. Normally, only police officers and others get to attend this course. But, I paid the fee in full and Daniel's letter did the rest."

"CVSA? As in Computerized Voice Stress Analyzer? A lie detector?"

"Yes, a very accurate lie detector. I've received the software, but I can't use the software until I pass the course. Then the school will send the activation codes for the software."

"That sounds like a reasonable enough request from the instructor/school. I want you to have Lynn file the paperwork, on behalf of the accused, asking the court to set reasonable bail. Lynn said you took some special pictures that won't be back for awhile?" asked Dale.

"Yes, the photos that I took were shot in infrared. There is only one photo lab in the entire country, besides law enforcement, that can develop the pictures and send them back to me."

"Daniel took me seriously in law school when I taught certain courses."

"Yes, he did, Your Honor."

The door to the outer office flew open. Melanie burst into the outer office. Dale and Jessica stood and walked into the outer office. Melanie was panting and in tears. She was holding up a piece of paperwork that said "Warrant to Search." Dale grabbed the search warrant and started reading it over as Jessica tried to calm down Melanie.

"Mrs. Thompson, what happened?" asked Dale.

"The FBI came back and started digging up my lawn, ransacking my home and they put handcuffs on my oldest son," she said as she started to cry.

"Did they find anything?" asked Dale as he handed the search warrant back to Melanie.

"No, I don't have anything to hide. But my oldest son is in handcuffs because he hit one of the agents with his gym bag."

"Did those agents announce who they were before entering your home? The search warrant does not say No Knock Search Warrant."

"I don't know; I wasn't home at the time."

"Are those agents still at your home?"

"Yes, I think so; can you help me?" Melanie asked.

"Miss Kim, please forward the phones to the answering service and let's follow Mrs. Thompson back to her home."

Dale, Mrs. Thompson and Jessica all drove to Mrs. Thompson's home in Silverton. The FBI agents were just finishing up their search. Jessica helped Dale out of the car. Dale walked over to the unmarked police car that had Melanie's oldest son in the backseat. The boy looked up at Dale and stopped moving around in the backseat. Dale looked around at some of the other agents that were just standing around the front door.

"Who is the agent in charge?" asked Dale as he started to drool.

"Who wants to know?" asked one of the agents on the porch.

Dale pulled out his Judge ID and opened it up for the agent to see.

"That boy in the backseat of this police car is my client and I wish to speak to him in private," said Dale as the drool dropped off of his chin. The agent handed him back his Judge ID which Dale put back into his left, rear pants pocket.

The agent opened the passenger-side car door and helped Dale into the car. The agent then shut the door.

"Hello, son, how are you doing?" asked Dale as he started to drool again.

"Fine, sir, but you're drooling all over yourself," said the kid.

"Thank you, son; I'll get you out of this in a few minutes. Did the agents announce who they were before or after they entered the home?" asked Dale as he wiped off the drool.

"After; all they said was 'FBI.' They scared me and my younger brother and I will admit, sir, that I hit the first FBI agent that came into the kitchen with my gym bag. It was the only thing I could grab for a weapon."

"Sounds like self-defense of yourself and your younger brother. Let me see what I can do; don't say a word to anyone."

Dale opened the car door up and stepped out of the car. He walked up to the front porch where Jessica and Melanie were standing. Melanie pointed to the man on her right as Special FBI Agent Larry Homes. Dale pulled out his ID and handed it to him. Larry looked it over and rolled his eyes back into his head as he handed the ID back to Dale. Dale put the ID back into his left, rear pants pocket.

"What can I do for you, Your Honor?" asked Larry.

"The juvenile in the police car, you need to let him go."

"Can't do that, Your Honor, he assaulted a federal law enforcement agent and will be locked up in Denver at the federal juvenile detention facility."

"He acted in self-defense of himself and his younger brother AFTER you and your boys entered the home WITHOUT announcing who you were. Besides, the search warrant didn't say No Knock across the top. You have to let him go."

"No dice, Your Honor, I'm still arresting him."

"You have, under your own FBI charter, no arrest powers except on federal property and only if the crime is committed in your presence. In order to arrest someone or search a person, place or thing, you need a U.S. Marshal to serve the warrants."

This last statement had Larry thinking.

"It's the kid's word against mine," said Larry, coolly.

"May I remind you that since there appears to be no U.S. Marshal present, the evidence you gathered during this search may be deemed inadmissible in a court of law? Also, under Title 18, United States Code, as Amended, you must follow the laws of the state you are operating in when making arrests."

"Are you telling me that I cannot arrest that kid in this state?"

"That's right, sir, ignorance is no excuse for breaking the law and I know that you are not above the law; remember section 1983 of Title 42 of the United States Code, as Amended, applies to you."

"What laws in this state am I breaking?"

"In accordance with Colorado Revised Statutes, Title 19, Juvenile Code, you are violating his rights. The charges, if any, will most likely be dropped if it gets to court."

"Your Honor, you're both lying and drooling."

"No, I'm not lying; check it out with the courthouse here in Silverton if you wish."

"I will."

Larry pulled out his cell phone and started making some phone calls. An hour later, he pulled the kid out of the police car. Larry then looked up on the porch at Dale and glared at him as he removed the kid's handcuffs. The kid ran into the house to make sure that his younger brother was okay. He then returned to the porch to see what else was going on. Larry looked up at the kid and pointed his right index finger at him, viciously shaking the finger at him.

"Son, it appears that your lawyer here has an in-depth knowledge of Colorado Law. He has been able to get the charges of assault dropped against you because of my ignorance of your state's laws. Be forewarned that the FBI will be watching your every move until we see fit to stop watching you."

"Thank you, Mr. Homes; are you finished with your search of my client's property?" asked Dale, wiping drool off of his chin.

"Yes."

"Then, I demand, sir, that you vacate the premises immediately so that my client can put her life back together from your intrusion."

Larry and his other agents stepped into their respective unmarked police cars and left. Special Agent Homes decided to flip-off Dale as they drove out of town. Dale, Melanie and Jessica walked inside the home, shut the door and locked it. Dale stared at the kid before speaking.

"The technicality that got you off the hook was a little known rule of law inside of Colorado Revised Statutes, Title 19, Juvenile Code. Don't let it happen again, you might not be so lucky."

"Thank you, Your Honor," said the kid, humbly.

"Well, Mrs. Thompson, I will be leaving here. I'll send you my bill."

"Thank you, Your Honor," she said as she let Dale and Jessica out the door. Melanie turned to face her kids.

"Let's see what the FBI took," she said as she prepared dinner.

Dale went home and Jessica and Lynn drove to Grand Junction to see Daniel. They found out from Daniel's temporary doctor that he was expected to make a full recovery in three months time.

CHAPTER 4

Monday morning arrived and Lynn opened the office early. She started a pot of coffee and began typing up the motions to suppress some of the evidence. Dale arrived a little after 8:30 a.m., having been driven to the office by Jill Halverston. He walked into the office, poured himself a cup of coffee, fixing it up the way he liked it, and walked into Daniel's inner office. Lynn followed him with the motions typed up, ready for his review.

"How is Daniel doing?" asked Dale, drooling.

"He's doing great, Your Honor. The attending doctor said he should be able to come home by Halloween."

"That is excellent news. Did you get the notes that Jessica left for you?"

"I did, Your Honor. I have typed up the motions to suppress some of the evidence; here they are," she said handing him the motions. He took them and set them down on the desktop.

"How well do you think you did on your LSAT exam?"

"Not well at all, Your Honor. It was hard to concentrate on some of the questions with Daniel in the hospital so far away. You know, he looked so peaceful sleeping there in the intensive care unit."

"I can understand that, Lynn. Let me review those motions and get them back out to you for changes," he said as he picked up the motions to begin the review process.

The final changes were made and Dale sent Lynn to the bank to get them notarized. Lynn returned to the office about 10:45 a.m.

Dale was busy reviewing more of Daniel's notes and sent Lynn to the courthouse with the motions. When she returned to the office, she filed the copies of the motions into the case file. She found Dale going through the evidence that was still left and comparing it to Daniel's notes. Dale looked up to see Lynn standing in the doorway.

"Lynn, does Daniel keep one notepad for all of his cases or does he use a separate notepad?" asked Dale as he slung drool all over the desktop.

"Daniel keeps a separate notepad for every one of his cases. He also keeps a smaller notepad with him for court use in his large briefcase. He sometimes keeps more than one small notepad in case the other one fills up," she replied, handing Dale a tissue.

"That large briefcase is still missing; right?" he asked wiping the drool off of himself and the desktop.

"Yes, is that an important fact to this case right now?"

"There was something on that notepad, I suspect, which caused those people to attack Daniel; how many notepads do you think Daniel had in that missing briefcase?"

"Three, I think."

"All right, we will surmise that Daniel has all three notepads in that briefcase. Do you know which cases Daniel was working on?"

"This case, with Mr. Berman, the Hawthorne case and I think one that was related to the Berman case in some manner."

"Related, what makes you think they are related?"

"Daniel was having Jessica gather some information about the CLO and the CFO of the company Mr. Berman works for at this time."

Dale was silent for a few minutes before speaking again.

"I think I may be having memory problems, but did you say Daniel keeps up to three notepads with each case?"

"Yes, Your Honor. One notepad stays here in the office and is permanently filed with the case when the case ends and he keeps up to two extra small notepads in his briefcase. These other notepads travel with him from office to court and back again."

"Does he do that with every case?"

"Yes, Your Honor, every case since I started working for him. Now, before that, I don't know because those case files are archived somewhere in Denver," she said, wondering why she had to keep repeating herself sometimes.

"It would appear that Daniel took me seriously in that course I taught at his law school. Lynn, that briefcase has to be found and soon. Since I am getting hungry, let's go eat."

Lynn forwarded the phones to the answering service and they went to eat at the local café. While they were eating their lunch, Jason walked into the café. He looked around and saw Lynn. He walked purposefully up to their table and took off his hat.

"Please excuse the intrusion, Your Honor, Lynn, but I called the office and the answering service said I might find you both here," said Jason.

"Not a problem, Marshal Beckman, what can we do for you?" asked Dale, wiping drool off of his chin and putting his sandwich down on the plate.

"I was able to locate Daniel's cell phone. The position was in Dolores County at the Fish Creek State Wildlife area. The Dolores County Sherriff's Department is bringing the cell phone back here today," said Jason.

"Any idea if the cell phone was with a large briefcase?" asked Lynn, trying to be calm about the possibility the briefcase and the cell phone were together.

"It was indeed, Lynn. When it gets here, I'll dust it for fingerprints and then you can claim it."

"Thank you, Marshal Beckman, that is very good news," said Dale, smiling.

Jason put his hat back on and left the café. Dale and Lynn finished off their lunches and left. When they arrived at the office, they found Linda waiting for them. She had a concerned look on her face. As they entered the office, Lynn unconsciously grabbed a pen from the top of her desk and the notepad they had been using for the Berman case. They all sat down in Daniel's inner office.

"Do you mind if Lynn takes notes, Linda?" asked Dale.

"No, in fact, I am here for several reasons, Your Honor. First, we have an appointment with Judge Bishop in his chambers on July 19th at 8:00 a.m. to discuss your motion to suppress evidence."

"Good and I thought you had come over here to discuss a plea bargain for my client," said Dale as he started drooling. This unnerved Linda a little.

"Even if I could, I know you would tell me no, just like Daniel would tell me no in most of his cases that I have prosecuted against him. The other thing I came to talk to you about is that guy who was arrested for Daniel's assault, is now being represented by a law firm out of Kansas City, Missouri."

"That's interesting, Linda. What is the name of this law firm?" asked Dale as he looked over at Lynn who was taking notes.

"The law firm is called, Dugan, Wainright and Lotus."

"Linda, take my advice, don't let them plea bargain this case; take it to trial. Linda, that law firm is the same law firm that Mr. Berman's employer uses and I have evidence that the law firm is bogus."

"So you think I am being duped?"

"Not really, I just think you need to be careful, that's all. Did you meet the lawyer from this law firm?"

"Not directly, I think only Nancy and the accused have seen the lawyer."

"Linda, this is only my gut feeling from being a former D.A. and judge; this guy will simply disappear if he is allowed bail."

"Then you would consider him a flight risk?"

"Yes and I feel he knows too much about Daniel's assault; he's going to either simply vanish or he will end up dead."

"I see, Your Honor. Let me get back to my office and check on all that information."

"Have a good day," said Dale as he drooled all over the desktop again, shaking Linda's hand as she left.

Linda left Daniel's office. Lynn remained with Dale for a few minutes before she put the notepad and pen down into her lap. Dale sat and stared at the wall for awhile before the telephone started to ring. Lynn answered the phone and then returned to the inner office.

"Who was that, Lynn?" asked Dale.

"It was Barry Goldman, Mr. Berman's employer. He was asking, if Bill made bail, if Bill could go back to work."

"If we can get reasonable bail set at the preliminary hearing, then Bill can go back to work."

"I kind of thought that was the case, however I told Barry you were the only one who could answer the question."

"Daniel has taught you well about being an attorney, Lynn. When you complete law school, you can count on my support."

"Thank you, Your Honor."

"Have you ever been in court when Daniel has selected the jury?"

"No, Your Honor, I was always hoping someday he would let me be there."

"Well, this case might be your lucky break. Do you have Mr. Goldman's number?"

"Yes, Your Honor," she said, handing Dale some tissues along with the phone number.

Dale wiped off his chin and dialed the number; Barry answered immediately.

"Yes, Your Honor, what can I do for you?" asked Barry after he saw who the Caller ID® said was calling.

"The answer to your question is yes. This surmises that I can get the judge to set reasonable bail."

"My company carries a policy for bailing out its employees to a maximum of five million dollars. But, this policy only covers non-capital crimes and the employee must elect to have their part of the insurance premium taken out of their paychecks each payday."

"Well, the crime is considered non-capital because it is not murder or mass murder, etc. I have never seen a judge, except in a few really bizarre cases, set bail for a manslaughter charge in excess of one hundred thousand dollars."

"What is the bail bond usually set at?"

"Twenty percent of the total bail set by the judge."

"My company will post bail on behalf of its employee. Mr. Berman is a good man and I don't think he did the crime either."

"Thank you, Mr. Goldman and while I have you on the phone, can I ask you how the trashcans and trash dumpsters are picked up?"

"Sure, what do you want to know?"

"How are the trashcans and trash dumpsters picked up by the trash removal company?"

"The trash truck enters the compound and uses some sort of giant hands or a forklift type device to pick the trashcans up and dump them into the back of the trash truck. The trash dumpsters are carried in and out of the compound via flatbed tractor-trailer."

"Does the driver or anyone else touch those trashcans or trash dumpsters?"

"No, the lids open automatically when someone steps on the sensor pads located in the concrete a few feet in front of the trashcans."

"Can I send my private investigator over there to dust down some of those trashcans for fingerprints?"

"Sure, Your Honor, I can meet her at the front gate in an hour."

"I'll make sure that she is there; goodbye," said Dale hanging up the phone. Lynn had quietly been taking notes.

"I'll call Jessica," said Lynn reaching for the phone.

Jessica went out and dusted the trashcans down for fingerprints. It took several attempts to get any useable fingerprints to show up. After a couple of hours, Jessica finally had some fingerprints that were clear and legible enough to lift. When she had lifted the prints and stored them in the fingerprint kit she had brought along, she left.

Jessica's next stop was to see Nancy; she had Nancy run the fingerprints through her Automated Fingerprint Identification System, or AFIS as it was called in the law enforcement community. Nancy had positively identified four of the six prints that Jessica had lifted as belonging to the deceased, Bob Quinest. Prints five and six were not in the AFIS database.

Jessica went to her office and typed up her report to go along with the four, positively identified fingerprints. She then went over to Daniel's office to drop off a copy of the report. Dale reviewed the report and turned to face Lynn.

"Lynn, let's all go home and get some good rest and would you please pick me up in the morning so that I am not late for court?" asked Dale.'

"Yes, Your Honor, but who is going to take you home tonight?" asked Lynn.

"Miss Kim, here," he said.

Lynn picked up Dale the next morning and they went to court. When they arrived at the courthouse, they found a lot of people waiting outside. There were reporters from some of the newspapers in the area and some of the employees from where Bill Berman worked that knew him. When Dale and Lynn cleared security and entered the courtroom, they found Bill sitting at the defendant's table.

They sat down and Sergio walked over to the table with eight tissue boxes. He returned to the table with four trashcans. He then walked back over to his post. The door to the left side of the front of the courtroom opened; Sergio stood up.

"All rise; criminal court for the 6th Judicial District in the town of Silverton, in San Juan County Colorado is now in session. The Honorable Judge Larry Bishop, presiding, over case number 14CR299, *The People v. Bill Berman,* on the charge of Manslaughter," said Sergio as everyone stood up.

Judge Bishop walked up the three small stairs to his chair on the bench. He put on his reading glasses and opened up the case file. He could hear the camera clicks and other devices going. He looked across the courtroom to the gallery area where the spectators were seated.

"You may be seated. Let me make this unmistakably clear to the spectators in the gallery, I do not allow cameras, cell phones with cameras or other recording devices in my courtroom. If you want to take pictures or shoot video footage, take it across the hallway into Judge Kyle Tillman's courtroom!" yelled Larry, banging his gavel down several times before the courtroom became quiet once again. Everyone sat down and the courtroom emptied out of some of the spectators.

"Thank you. Now, in the case of *The People v. Bill Berman,* case number 14CR299, this is the preliminary hearing. Is the prosecution ready?" asked Larry.

"We are, Your Honor," said Linda, standing up and then sitting back down.

"So noted. Is defense counsel ready?"

"We are, Your Honor," said Dale standing up and looking past Judge Bishop before sitting back down.

"So noted. Prosecution, are you ready with your argument for or against setting bail?"

"We are ready, Your Honor," she replied as she stood up.

"Very well, proceed," said Larry as he started to take notes.

"Thank you, Your Honor. We request that bail be denied for the defendant. This is due to his previous brush with federal law enforcement personnel. The defendant has only a few ties to this community. He has no wife, girlfriend, boyfriend, house, kids or pets to keep him here; in short, a flight risk," said Linda as she sat back down.

"So noted. Is defense counsel ready with their arguments?"

"We are ready, Your Honor," said Dale, standing up with tissue in his right hand.

"Very well, proceed."

Dale wiped the drool off of his chin and tossed the tissue into one of the trashcans near him. He cleared his throat and looked a little past Judge Bishop out the window behind Sergio's desk.

"Your Honor, my client is not a flight risk. Yes, my client has few permanent ties to this community, but he has a job he enjoys doing. He has an employer who desperately needs him to return to work to cut down on the massive overtime that is occurring at his place of employment because of my client's continued absence. This same employer believes so highly in my client, this employer is willing to post bail on my client's behalf as long as it is reasonable," said Dale as he started drooling again.

"So noted. Is defense counsel asking this court to set reasonable bail for the defendant?" asked Larry.

"Yes, Your Honor, we are asking this court to set reasonable bail," replied Dale, slinging spit all over the defendant's tabletop.

"So noted. This court cannot grant a personal recognizance bond due to the nature of the charge."

"Objection, Your Honor, The People consider him a flight risk," said Linda, standing up and sitting back down again.

"Sustained, for now, prosecution," said Larry.

"I object, Your Honor. If my client is such a flight risk, then can the prosecution explain to defense counsel and this court why my client's employer is not only present in the back of the courtroom, but is willing to make sure that my client gets back to work where my client can be monitored by cameras and keycards? I hardly think that makes my client a flight risk," said Dale, spitting in the direction of Linda as he sat back down.

"Is the employer present in the gallery?" asked Larry.

Barry stood up and raised his right hand as he walked up to the swinging gate entrance to the front of the courtroom.

"I am, Your Honor. The defendant is desperately needed back at work to cut down on the overtime issues that I am having due to his absence. I will ensure that the defendant is monitored while at work by cameras and keycards as well as posting the defendant's reasonable bail bond if he is given one by this court. The defendant is a great employee that is missed by his fellow security officers and employees at the facility," said Barry.

"What is your name and who do you work for?" asked Larry.

"My name is Barry Goldman and I am the Chief Security Officer of Rocky Mountain Security Services."

"How long has the defendant been your employee?"

"More than five years, Your Honor."

"Up until this incident, did you ever have any disciplinary problems with the defendant?" asked Larry.

"Only one, Your Honor, in the beginning, but none since then; he is a model employee that everyone likes and trusts at the facility."

"So noted. Does the prosecution have any other evidence to present to this court to deny bail on the basis of the defendant being a flight risk?"

"None, Your Honor," said Linda while she remained seated.

"Very well, this court is in recess for ten minutes," said Larry, banging his gavel down.

Larry exited the courtroom, taking off his reading glasses and putting them into his upper shirt pocket under his robe. Larry returned ten minutes later and had Sergio skip the usual prefunctionaries. He went directly to his seat on the bench and put on his reading glasses as he opened up the case file again.

"Before this court decides whether or not to grant or deny bail to the defendant, this court would like to know when the defendant's primary attorney will be available for trial?" asked Larry.

Dale wiped drool off of his chin once again and turned to face Lynn who gave him the answer.

"Your Honor, Daniel is scheduled to be released from the hospital on Halloween of this year," said Dale.

"So noted. This court is going to grant bail to the defendant in the amount of seventy-five thousand dollars. The trial will begin November 14th of this year," said Larry banging down his gavel, taking off his reading glasses, setting them down on the bench while closing up the case file.

CHAPTER 5

The briefcase was returned to Lynn. Jason was very careful to lift only the really good fingerprints from the briefcase. Jason then took those fingerprints to Nancy so that they could compare them. After running the prints through Nancy's AFIS system, the computer concluded that the fingerprints taken off of the briefcase matched the person in custody's entire left hand. Nancy called Linda to let her know what they had found.

Linda was very pleased with the information and proceeded with the list of charges she had waiting for the man. When the man went for his preliminary hearing, Linda was able to get bail denied for him. After a few days in Nancy's jailhouse, he decided to plead guilty to the charge that Linda had offered him; First Degree Assault with a possible prison term of thirty years to life.

Jessica went off to her school and Lynn drove to Grand Junction every weekend to see Daniel. While Jessica was in the school, Lynn would call her periodically to give her updates on Daniel's condition. By the time Jessica returned from her school, Daniel was fully awake and asking Lynn about what had been going on since he entered the hospital. Lynn filled him in on as many details as she could remember.

When the man's sentencing date arrived, Judge Kyle Tillman gave the man a forty-five year prison sentence plus restitution. Lynn had been told by Linda when the sentencing hearing would be and since Daniel was awake, Judge Kyle Tillman allowed Daniel to listen in on the hearing. Daniel was very pleased with the outcome of the hearing and went to physical therapy after he hung up the phone.

Lynn returned to the office after leaving the courthouse in Silverton, to find Jessica waiting for her. Jessica had received the photos taken at the crime scene. The pictures showed evidence of dried, human blood of an unknown type as well as a possible bullet hole in the lower part of the back of the elevator's false paneling. When the other pictures were looked at that had been taken on the top of the elevator car, they showed larger quantities of dried, human blood. This new evidence seemed to lend more support of the theory that the blood belonged to the person who had shot Bill and then used the elevator shaft to escape.

The day had finally arrived for the hearing, in Judge Bishop's chambers, on the motion to suppress evidence. There was much discussion and back and forth debating amongst the parties. When the final rebuttal had finished being given, Judge Bishop said he would issue his decision in five business days. Daniel was not happy about having to wait, but wait was all he could do for the moment.

Melanie was allowed to continue to work, for the time being. She was asked every morning about taking the polygraph test. She refused each time, politely, saying that they could speak to her lawyer about the polygraph test. Melanie was getting more and more cash counts and cash audits than usual. She took them all in stride and never really worried about anything.

Lynn walked into the office seven business days later to find an envelope in the stack of mail from Judge Bishop's office. She didn't open the letter up, but took it into Dale for him to open it up and read it. He wiped drool off of his chin and opened the letter up, scanned it over quickly and put it back into the envelope.

He handed the letter back to Lynn and told her to call Daniel. Lynn called Daniel only to find out he was in physical therapy. The duty nurse said she would have Daniel call Lynn when he returned from physical therapy. Daniel called Lynn back after he ate his lunch.

"What's the big news, Lynn?" asked Daniel.

"The motion to suppress evidence ruling has been returned by His Honor Judge Bishop."

"What was the ruling?" asked Daniel excitedly.

Lynn picked up the letter so she could read it to him over the phone.

"The motion to suppress the requested evidence has been granted."

"That is good news, Lynn; anything new with Melanie?"

"Nothing recently; when are you coming home?" she asked, changing the subject as fast as she could.

"Looks like Halloween is the magical date. I will surmise that you will be here to pick me up; right?"

"Myself and Jessica; goodbye," said Lynn as she hung up the phone.

The day before Lynn and Jessica went to pick up Daniel, the news reporter from the *Ironton Gazette,* Mary Jean, entered Daniel's office. Lynn looked up a little concerned at first, due to the late hour, but Lynn greeted Mary anyway.

"Please take these three editions of the newspaper with the compliments of the editor of the *Ironton Gazette,"* Mary said handing Lynn three copies of the October 31st edition.

"Thank you and is one of these copies for Daniel?" asked Lynn, who already knew the answer.

"Yes; goodbye," she said as she left the office quickly.

Lynn opened up the newspaper. The front-page headline was very nice to read: "WELCOME HOME ATTORNEY DANIEL MARCOS!" Lynn called Jessica and they drove to Grand Junction that Wednesday night. The office was closed the next day and a storm system had moved into the San Juan Mountains during the night. The storm system had already started dropping snow on the San Juans. Daniel read the newspaper as they all drove into the snowstorm.

In Montrose, Colorado, the sunlight of the afternoon was cut down to almost nothing. The snow flakes started out small as Lynn turned onto Highway 550. Lynn was thankful for Jessica's four-wheel drive vehicle. They had to stop and refuel in Ouray, Colorado before beginning the final leg of the drive to Ironton. The road conditions started getting progressively worse; the snowflakes were getting bigger and wetter. As they approached one of the most formidable and dangerous mountain passes in the world, visibility was almost zero.

Suddenly, flashing lights and a siren sounded as they approached the gate for closing the pass if conditions were unfavorable for driving. Lynn looked over to her right at the flashing sign on the side of the road. The sign said: "RED MOUNTAIN PASS CLOSED." Lynn stopped the car as the flashing lights pulled up alongside Lynn's side of the car. Lynn rolled down the driver's side window.

"I will surmise that one of the passengers is Attorney Daniel Marcos; welcome home Mr. Marcos. Currently, Red Mountain Pass is closed, but I want you to put the vehicle into the four-wheel drive, four LOW range. Put on chains, if you have them and follow the snowplow. DO NOT lose sight of the snowplow."

"Thank you Trooper, we will do what you have instructed us to do," said Lynn putting the car into the four LOW range. They all exited the vehicle and grabbed the chains out of the back of Jessica's car.

Lynn, Jessica and even Daniel helped put the chains on the car. They all stepped back into the car and started to follow the snowplow. As they drove past the flashing sign, Trooper Davis closed the gate arm and locked it shut. Daniel and Jessica looked out the partially fogged-over windows. As they continued towards the summit at 11,018 feet above sea level, the snow was over the top of the car. As they continued to follow the snowplow, they all could see that the snow was now half way up the door of the snowplow.

They finally reached the first of the two summits that Red Mountain Pass has and the visibility was zero. The snow was being driven at a straight angle by the high winds at that elevation. Lynn kept a tight grip on the steering wheel as well as both eyes on the alternate flashing blue and yellow strobe lights. Two hours later, they reached the other side, safely. The weather was a little different in Silverton.

As they turned off of the main highway and onto the main street of Silverton, the Silverton Town Marshal met them. She escorted them through town to the outskirts of the town where Lynn turned onto Highway 550A. There were lots of people holding up signs welcoming Daniel home. When they arrived at the outskirts of Ironton, Jason met them.

"Welcome home, Mr. Marcos; I believe that you will find the Ironton Café is still open for business," said Jason as he waved his right hand above his head.

Some volunteers, mostly former clients of Daniel's, let go of the ropes that they had been holding and a big banner unfurled in the wind and light snow that was beginning to fall. The banner said, "WELCOME HOME ATTORNEY DANIEL MARCOS ESQUIRE! FROM THE TOWN OF IRONTON." The mayor and the city council of Ironton along with the Assistant Ironton Town Marshal, Dale and a few other hardy Ironton residents welcomed Daniel back as well. Daniel thanked them all for their support. Daniel, Lynn and Jessica all had dinner at the café where Daniel tried to pay for the bill. The café owner and part time chef refused to take the money.

For Daniel it was enough to be home. He ate all he could and had to take some of it home for later. The pharmacy in Silverton filled his various prescriptions. Daniel had Lynn check into the only hotel in Silverton for the night, since he knew that getting to Telluride was out of the question. Daniel went home to find everything was neatly taken care of during his absence. Lynn had done his laundry, dusted things down, forwarded the phone to the office and had organized his mail and newspapers. He went to bed after taking a shower.

Friday morning, he went to the hotel were Lynn was located and she drove them both to work. She started a pot of coffee and drove the car back to Silverton to Jessica. Jessica drove Lynn back to the office. Shortly after Lynn entered the office, Jason Beckman showed up with Melanie's oldest son in the back of his patrol car. Marshal Beckman grabbed a hold of the kid and assisted him out of the backseat. Daniel could hear some yelling and screaming. As he looked out the front door of his office, Daniel smiled.

"Lynn, it appears we have a possible new client arriving and isn't it nice that Marshal Beckman personally delivered him to me so that I wouldn't have to walk all the way to the marshal's office," said Daniel.

Lynn looked up at the person who was being brought into the office and her mouth dropped open.

"Oh my Lord, that is Melanie's oldest son," said Lynn, gasping a little.

"Well, fortunate for him he is my client."

The door opened and Marshal Beckman threw Melanie's oldest son into one of the office chairs. Daniel could see that the kid was in handcuffs and that his clothes were ruffled up a bit. Daniel also saw the bloody nose and fat lip.

"What can I do for you, Marshal Beckman?" asked Daniel.

"I arrested this kid here and I plan on charging him with assault. The only thing he told me was that you were his lawyer and he won't talk to me."

"I can understand you're frustration, Marshal Beckman, with my juvenile client. I will confirm that this person is my client. Now, if you will kindly step into my more private office, we can discuss the charge."

Marshal Beckman looked at Daniel suspiciously at first before turning to face Lynn.

"Do you have the retainer receipt?" asked Jason.

"I do, Marshal Beckman, but without either a subpoena deuces tecum or a seizure warrant for the retainer receipt, I cannot give it to you. It might violate the attorney/client privilege," she said as she pulled up Melanie's file, covered over Melanie's first name and showed the file to Jason.

Jason looked it over and turned to face Daniel.

"I'm sorry, Marshal Beckman, but my client's case file or files are attorney/client privilege protected," said Daniel, smiling.

"I thought I would ask anyway. This juvenile client of yours says you have advised him of his Constitutional rights; is that true?"

"My client has been advised of his Constitutional rights. In fact, I routinely advise my clients of their Constitutional rights and I have them sign a form stating such."

Jason turned to face the kid.

"Did you sign a form like that, son?"

"Yes, sir, I did."

"*The kid is not as dumb as he looks. I am impressed,*" said Daniel to himself.

"Now, Marshal Beckman, if you will come into my private office, we can talk. Lynn, please keep an eye on my client."

"Will do, Daniel."

Marshal Beckman and Daniel stepped into Daniel's private, inner office. Daniel shut the door and sat down in the chair at his desk. Marshal Beckman took off his hat and set it down on the desktop.

"Thank you, Marshal Beckman, for returning my personal property to me and for assisting Linda in prosecuting that person who assaulted me," said Daniel.

"You're welcome, Daniel. Now, about your juvenile client."

"Well, I would want to ask a few questions. First, did you see my client commit the assault?"

"No."

"Second, may I see your seizure warrant for my client's body?"

"I don't have one, Daniel; I am sorry."

"I see, so you arrested my client without physically seeing him commit the crime that you are charging him with; now you tell me you don't have a seizure warrant for my client's body? Do you know, Marshal Beckman, that you violated my client's 4th, 5th and 14th Amendment rights, as well as his rights under Colorado Revised Statutes, Title 19, Juvenile Code? Can we just dispense with the bull and get down to the meat of the matter?"

"All right, if I tell you what happened, can I get a copy of the paperwork that your client signed?"

Daniel sat back in his chair a little and saw that the light was on under the INTERCOM button.

"Sure, Marshal Beckman, you can pick up a copy of my client's advisement of his Constitutional rights and the retainer receipt on the way out the door," said Daniel as the light went out as he looked straight at Marshal Beckman.

"Your client has alleged that he was first verbally harassed before being physically assaulted by some of his classmates at the high school."

"Let me guess, Marshal Beckman, those kids' parents work with my client's mother, Melanie Thompson, at the bank, don't they?" asked Daniel.

"Yes, how did you know?"

"A logical guess based upon my client's last name. Now, how many other kids were involved with this altercation?"

"Four other kids plus three witnesses."

"Are they all over the age of ten?"

"Yes."

"Do you know who threw the first punch?"

"Not exactly, all I have are the witness statements, which don't exactly match one hundred percent and the victims' statements."

"My client does have a right to claim self-defense against your charge of assault. Besides, there were four other kids involved; I don't like a four to one fight, Marshal Beckman."

"So, are you saying I should charge the victims as well as the kid?"

"Yes, if they can't get their stories straight. I think you should consider charging them with Disorderly Conduct, C.R.S. 18-9-106, Inciting a Riot, C.R.S. 18-9-102 or maybe a Bias Motivated Crime, C.R.S. 18-9-121."

"How did you come up with the inciting a riot charge?"

"C.R.S. 18-9-102, Inciting a Riot only requires five people organized into lawlessness. At the very least, you might want to consider charging the witnesses with being an accessory to and after the fact. By the way, does my client have a criminal record in any state that you found while doing a records check on him?"

"No, your client appears to be a clean person."

"Then why start charging him with something that he may not have done?"

"I see what you mean; I'll drop the charges if I can get a copy of that paperwork on the way out the door?" said Jason as he grabbed his hat, put it on his head and hitched up his duty belt. Daniel opened the office door.

"Thank you, Marshal Beckman. Now, if you will take off the handcuffs from my client, Lynn will give you the information you asked for," said Daniel as Jason took off the handcuffs.

Daniel saw Lynn hand Jason a couple of pieces of paper. There were signatures on all of the pieces of paper. Jason looked over the paperwork and then turned to face the kid.

"Is this your signature?" asked Jason pointing at the bottom of the first piece of paperwork.

"Yes, sir, it is."

"Marshal Beckman, could you give my client a ride back to school, please?" asked Daniel, nicely.

"Sure, I will be waiting at my patrol car."

Jason left the office. Daniel turned to face the kid.

"All I want to know is, who threw the first punch and don't lie to me."

"The bank manger's son."

"Very well, now you can go back to school."

The kid left and Daniel turned to see Lynn getting off the phone. She had taken some notes and handed the notes to Daniel. Daniel read over the notes and smiled.

"Lynn, let's go have lunch and meet my client at Danny's office."

"The private investigator up here?"

"Yes, he wants to administer the lie detector test to my client and I think we both should be there."

CHAPTER 6

Daniel and Lynn went to lunch. After they finished off lunch, Daniel took his painkillers, anti-inflammatory and antibiotics. They walked into the private investigator's office. Daniel found Melanie sitting quietly in a chair being hooked up to the polygraph machine. When Daniel saw the old polygraph machine, he didn't like it one bit; Daniel walked into the room.

"Before you interrogate my client, I will advise her of her rights," said Daniel getting a funny look from Danny.

Daniel turned to face Melanie.

"Sure, counselor, you do whatever you want," he said smiling.

"Mrs. Melanie Thompson, as your attorney, I must advise you of your legal rights. Under the Employee Polygraph Protection Act of 1988 and as amended in 2010, the polygraph test results are not admissible in criminal court. Do you understand this right as I have explained it to you?"

"Yes, Mr. Marcos, I understand," replied Melanie.

"You have the right to have another type of polygraph test done, using the same questions. Do you understand this right as I have explained it to you?"

"Yes."

"Do you wish to exercise your right to have this other type of polygraph test done, at your expense, using the same questions?" asked Daniel, winking his right eye.

"Yes, Mr. Marcos, I wish to have another type of polygraph test administered to me, using the same questions and at my own expense."

"Good, I need a copy of the questions you are going to ask my client," said Daniel as he turned to face Danny.

"Sorry, I'm not going to give you the questions," said Danny.

"Very well, then, this polygraph test is over. Mrs. Thompson, the polygraph test you were about to be given is known to be less than ten percent accurate. It is also known that there are at least two hundred and fifty ways to defeat this type of polygraph test."

"No liar has ever passed one of my tests. Besides, Mrs. Thompson, that other type of polygraph test he told you about is called a CVSA, or Computerized Voice Stress Analyzer. It is very expensive and there's no way you can get one before the close of business today," said Danny.

"Mrs. Thompson, my private investigator can give you the CVSA in about an hour as long as I have a list of the questions."

"Okay, counselor, I will give you a copy of the list of questions," he said, handing Daniel a list of seventy-five questions.

"Mrs. Thompson, I will be waiting for you outside," said Daniel as he took the list of questions and handed them to Lynn. Lynn pulled out her cell phone and made the call to Jessica.

Jessica set up her equipment and drove to the other private investigator's office. She picked up the list of questions and Mrs. Thompson. Daniel agreed to provide a copy of the CVSA results to Danny for his records. Once Melanie was done with the CVSA test, Jessica took her home. Daniel and Lynn had returned to the office where Daniel was filled in on the latest developments of the Berman case. After Daniel had read over the notes that Dale had written down, he received a phone call from his insurance agent. The agent stated to Daniel that the vehicle was too badly damaged to be economically repaired, so the insurance company was sending Daniel a check to go get another car.

Now Daniel was without a car, so he had Lynn agree to pick him up at his house and drop him off at his house until he could get another car with the insurance check.

Lynn told Daniel that he was on the prosecutions' witness list. Daniel wasn't happy about it, but he knew that this was one tactic that Linda might use to discredit him and his client in front of a jury. That night, after he ate dinner and took his medicine again, he walked to Melanie's house to see her. Her youngest son opened the door and smiled at Daniel.

"Is your mother home?" asked Daniel, nicely.

"Yeah; mommy, that lawyer's here and he's cute!" he yelled.

A moment later, Melanie appeared at the door. She was shaking a little and seemed very nervous. She ushered Daniel into the living room where he met her second oldest son. He was playing an electronic game of fishing. Daniel smiled and then followed Melanie into the kitchen.

"I'm sorry about what Todd said earlier," said Melanie, rather embarrassed.

"So, Todd is his name. Don't worry about it; I get complimented like that all the time. Can I see your oldest son's room?" asked Daniel, politely.

"David's room? Sure," she said, taking Daniel upstairs to see the room.

She opened the door and Daniel looked around to see fishing gear, camping gear, backpacks and what appeared to be airbrushing equipment. Daniel then saw all of the mounts of the fish that David had caught. There was a large specimen of a Bluegill, a Tilapia, a channel catfish and a very large specimen of a northern pike. He closed the door and they returned to the kitchen where they talked.

"Did David taxidermy all those fish himself?" asked Daniel as he started to take notes on a small notepad and pen he kept in the right, front jacket pocket.

"Not exactly, he took a picture of the fish before he ate it of course. He then used some of the money from doing odd jobs, in the other places we lived in Colorado before coming here and he ordered fiberglass molds out of a taxidermy catalog he still gets. He would then spend hours carefully painting the fish mold."

"Well, that explains the airbrush equipment I saw in the left corner of the room. When your case is over, I'll take the boys all fishing at a place called John Martin Reservoir in Baca County. I have a boat and the boys can all try to catch a tiger muskie," said

Daniel as he had been hearing the breathing sounds of her middle boy from around the corner.

"That would be great, Mr. Marcos. I think the boys would really enjoy that fishing trip. So, you think we are headed for a trial then?"

"Oh, yes and your middle boy has been listening to our entire conversation including my statement about going fishing from around the corner," said Daniel pointing with his left thumb to the corner where the kitchen and the living room came together.

Melanie stood up from the kitchen table as Daniel put up the notepad and pen.

"Seth! Have you been listening to our conversation?" asked Melanie.

Seth came from around the corner.

"Not all of it, well except for the part about the boat and fishing. Mr. Marcos, how did you know where I was standing?" asked Seth.

"I could hear you breathing. I will keep my promise to you, Todd and David; goodnight Mrs. Thompson."

"Goodnight, Mr. Marcos; by the way, they put me on paid administrative leave for now."

"Good, why don't you come see me in court on Monday?"

"I will."

Daniel walked home, took a shower and went to bed. Daniel woke up at his usual time and did a light workout. He knew that it would be some time before he was fully recovered. He ate breakfast, sorted through some of the mail and backlog of newspapers before Lynn arrived to pick him up for work. They arrived at work to find a large, plain white envelope sitting on the floor underneath the mail slot. Lynn carefully opened the door. Daniel picked up the envelope and carefully held it up to the light that was directly in front of him.

The outline of the envelope's contents indicated a solid, rectangular shaped object inside. Daniel didn't see any wires or other items in the outline. He carefully squeezed the envelope and didn't feel anything stiff inside like a battery pack. He looked over at Lynn who had already pulled out a pair of scissors from her desktop container.

"Lynn, I don't see any trip wires and I don't feel any battery packs, so I can safely say it isn't a letter bomb. I want you to carefully cut the top off of the envelope while I hold it together just in case there is a hidden trip wire," said Daniel.

Lynn carefully cut the top off of the envelope. She then quickly moved out from behind her desk. Carefully Daniel dumped the contents out onto her desktop. They looked down at the stack of money that was now on the desktop. The money was wrapped up in a piece of paper. The piece of paper had the Ironton Town Bank and Trust's name, logo and address on it. On the front of the piece of paper it simply said, "For legal fees, M.T." Daniel looked at the stack of money and started going through it.

There were two-hundred and forty-two, $20.00 bills and one $10.00 bill in the stack. Daniel looked at the bills a little closer now; all of them, with the exception of the $10.00 bill, were in sequential order. They were all 1981 Series A's, appeared new and looked like they had just come off the printing press yesterday. Daniel looked up at Lynn.

"Looks like someone has paid for Melanie Thompson's legal fees. Lynn, send Melanie a bill and show on the bill that the retainer was paid for in full and then lock the money up in the safe in the basement."

"Will do, Daniel; what else is going to happen on this case?"

"I don't know, so be prepared. Now, I'm going into my office and I'm going to prepare my opening statements for Monday."

"I'll make sure that you are not unnecessarily bothered."

"Thank you, Lynn."

Daniel began making his notes out as to what he wanted to say during his opening statements. Next, he took a short nap in his office chair because the painkillers had taken full effect. After he woke up from his nap, he poured himself a cup of coffee, fixed it the way he liked it and went back to his inner office. After he had reread the police reports, coroner's findings and other evidence, Daniel was able to formulate a better picture of what happened that night. Jessica showed up about lunchtime with the results of the CVSA test; Lynn showed her right into Daniel's inner office, closing the door behind her.

"Well, Jessica, is my client, Melanie Thompson, a liar or perhaps a good used car salesman or perhaps even a politician?" asked Daniel as he looked over her official report. They both laughed a little.

"Melanie Thompson, in my opinion and as backed up by my instructor at the school I recently attended, is telling the truth. This is based upon the three control questions I asked her and the questions that were provided to me by you."

"Good job, make sure that Lynn pays you for your services. You and Lynn go to lunch and then you both can help me identify defense exhibits."

"See you after lunch and I personally delivered a copy of the CVSA test results to the other private investigator."

"Good girl."

Daniel finished off every leftover in the refrigerator. He washed the dishes and put them up to dry in the dish rack that was to the left of the sink. He went back to his inner office and called Nancy.

"I'm sorry, Mr. Marcos, Nancy is out on patrol. Let me connect you with her on her cell phone," said the assistant town marshal as he connected Daniel's phone call with Nancy's cell phone; Nancy answered after the first ring.

"Yes, Daniel, what can I do for you?" she asked excitedly because the patrol was very boring.

"I have a couple of questions for you."

"Go ahead, Daniel."

"When you were going through Mr. Quinest's personal effects, did you come across any clothing items that had blood on them?"

"If you're referring to the inventory of the deceased's property, yes, I did find some bloody gauze wraps, a couple pairs of socks and a pair of what appeared to me to be black, BDU type pants."

"I'm guessing that by the term BDU, you mean Battle Dress Uniform; right?"

"That's right."

"That's okay; I just wanted to make sure we were both talking about the same thing. Now, did you find any shoes or boots?"

"No, I sure didn't find anything like that Daniel; sorry."

"That's okay; did you inventory Mr. Quinest's car?"

"No, but the car is still in my impound lot because the caretakers of the estate of the deceased didn't want to take it with them; why?"

"I believe if you inventory the contents of the car, I suspect you will find a pair of blood soaked boots or shoes. On the front toe part of one of those shoes, I believe you will find blood on it."

"Daniel, we are both professionals in our own right. Just tell me what I am looking for and I'll find it if the evidence is there."

"If you find a bloody shoe, the blood on the front toe part of that shoe will most likely match my client's blood type. I suggest that you run the blood typing test to prove this and it will prove that Mr. Quinest was the one who was on the property, shot my client and then kicked my client as a final insult."

"Okay, I'll have my assistant town marshal do the inventory tonight; goodbye."

"Thank you and goodbye."

Jessica and Lynn returned to the office after lunch. They helped Daniel with marking the defense exhibits. After Lynn, Jessica and Daniel had loaded all the evidence into Jessica's car, Lynn drove the evidence down to Judge Bishop's courtroom. The Bailiff helped unload the car and they all returned to the office. Daniel called the highway patrol to find out if Red Mountain Pass was open yet so that Lynn could get home. The pass was open, but it required studded snow tires and chains. Daniel called them both into the office.

"Lynn, would you give Jessica your car keys and Jessica would you give Lynn your car keys, please? I called the highway patrol; they just reopened Red Mountain Pass, but there are restrictions on driving the pass. Lynn, I suggest that you leave really early Monday morning, because I need you in court, of course. Now, Jessica, I need to talk to you," said Daniel pulling out his wallet and handing Lynn some money.

The women exchanged car keys. Jessica walked into Daniel's inner office after Lynn had left. Daniel sat down at his desk and spread out the infrared photos on the desktop. Jessica sat quietly while Daniel sorted out the pictures in numerical order as well as date and time stamp. He picked up her report which the prosecution already had a copy of.

"Jessica, you say in your report here that photos two through ten are of blood spots and a possible bullet hole. How can you prove this to the jury without showing favoritism to me?" asked Daniel.

"Oh, that's an easy one, Daniel. I sprayed down the inside of the elevator with a combination of Luminol® for detecting the presence of human blood, whether fresh or not. However, since Luminol® doesn't react with gunshot residue, I used the Nitrate spray."

"Wouldn't one test cancel out the other one?"

"No, since the chemicals are of two totally different types, they can be used together without crossing over each other. It is a known fact that Nitrate doesn't react to blood, but Luminol® will and vice versa."

"What did you spray the top of the elevator with that are photos twelve through eighteen?"

"I used only Luminol® on top."

"Good girl, now my biggest question to you is, how certain are you of the positive Nitrate test on the small hole in the back of the elevator, in photo twenty-two, being a bullet hole?"

"Very positive, Daniel."

"Are you more than half positive of that fact?"

"More than ninety percent certain, Daniel."

"Okay, good girl, I'll see you in court on Monday morning."

Jessica left the office and drove to her office in Silverton. Daniel left his office a few minutes later and walked down the street to the Ironton Town Marshal's office. Jill Halverston, the Assistant Town Marshal, was getting ready to go out on patrol and offered Daniel a ride home. As Daniel was getting out of the patrol car, he turned to face Jill.

"Jill, who is the duty judge on call tonight?" he asked.

"I believe it is Judge Kyle Tillman."

"Could you have him call me on my cell phone, please?"

"Sure, Daniel and have a good evening," she said as she drove off.

Daniel walked into his house and locked the front door. He turned on his computer and started clearing up his backlog of emails. When he was down to the last ten days of emails, he shut off his computer. Next, he went through his regular email and newspapers. Lastly, he began to shred the junk mail. When he had emptied the paper shredder for the fifth time, he stopped shredding. As he walked down the stairs into his living room, his cell phone started ringing.

"Hello?" asked Daniel.

"Daniel, welcome home, this is Judge Kyle Tillman. What can I do for you?" he asked politely.

"Your Honor, I know in the past I have asked for some unusual things," Daniel started to say, but Judge Kyle Tillman cut him off.

"Those unusual things have almost always turned out to be the saving graces for your clients. What do you need?"

"I need a search warrant and I would like it to be served tonight if possible. If not, can it be served by Sunday night at the latest?"

"Sure, Daniel, not a problem; I will pull out the search warrant right now and await you to either fax or email me the affidavit. I won't have to ask for it to be notarized because everyone on the nightshift tonight with me knows you well."

"Thank you, Your Honor; goodbye."

Daniel hung up his phone and typed up the affidavit which he sent to Judge Kyle Tillman at his email address. Daniel then used his home phone to call Nancy Gills to see what she had going on that night. Nancy told Daniel that she was too busy with some drunk and disorderlies to handle the search tonight. She suggested contacting the San Juan County Sheriff's Department. He hung up his phone and called the San Juan County Sheriff's Department.

"Thank you for calling the San Juan County Sheriff's Department. This is Deputy Brunoe speaking; how can I help you?" he asked.

"Deputy Brunoe, this is Attorney Daniel Marcos calling, is Deputy Holds on duty tonight?"

"Yes, she's standing right in front of me," said Brunoe as he handed Gilda the phone receiver.

"Hello?" she asked.

"Deputy Holds, this is Attorney Daniel Marcos, I need to email you an affidavit for a search warrant; what is your email address?"

"You can call me Gilda and my email address is G.Holds@ SJCSO.gov."

"Hold on," said Daniel as he hit the SEND key on his computer. A few seconds later, Gilda received the emailed affidavit.

"Okay, Daniel, I received your email; who is the duty judge?"

"Judge Kyle Tillman and I suspect he has already signed the search warrant and is probably waiting for you. He told me that he didn't need the affidavit notarized because he and his night staff know me well enough."

"All right, am I going to need help with this search of yours?"

"I am sure that I can get the duty security force personnel and the duty maintenance personnel to assist you with your search."

"Okay and I will call you if I, or we, find what I am, or we are, looking for; fair enough?"

"I'll be waiting with bated breath; goodbye."

Gilda hung up the phone. Daniel called Barry and told him what was about to happen. Barry said he would assist with the search in any way possible. He notified the facility security force personnel and the duty maintenance personnel to be ready to assist in any way that law enforcement personnel directed them. Daniel hung up his phone and started thinking about what he was going to have for dinner. It was about 8:00 p.m. when someone knocked on Daniel's front door. Keeping his left foot braced up against the door, he cautiously opened it a crack to see who it was standing on the front porch.

"Mr. Marcos, I thought you might be hungry, so I brought you a plate of home cooked food," said Melanie as she presented a plate of food for him to look over and it looked really good from his point of view.

"Why, thank you, Mrs. Thompson and please come inside; where are the boys?" asked Daniel as he opened the door to let her inside.

"They are in Durango with their grandparents for the weekend."

They had dinner and a quiet conversation. Daniel took all of his drugs and they went to bed together. Daniel's cell phone started ringing around 2:00 a.m. on a Saturday morning. Daniel answered his cell phone, still a little groggy from the painkillers.

"Hello?" asked Daniel, slurring his words a little.

"Daniel, this is Gilda and sorry for the early hour," she said.

"I gather you found something?"

"Yes, a badly deformed bullet in a crawlspace in the bottom of the elevator shaft. A place the maintenance personnel here call the pit sword room."

"Good work, Gilda. Did you send that bullet off to Garth Smith, yet?"

"Sure did; he should get it by Monday morning for analysis."

"Again, Gilda, good work by everyone down there," Daniel said as he hung up his phone and went back to sleep.

CHAPTER 7

Monday morning arrived for Daniel, Lynn, Jessica, Mr. Berman and twelve prospective jurors who would determine his client's fate. Daniel was picked up by Lynn and they drove directly to the courthouse. They cleared security and went directly to the courtroom. The Bailiff smiled when Daniel and Lynn walked into the courtroom. Daniel checked to see that all of his evidence was neatly arranged on the evidence table.

The Bailiff had set up the DVD player with a widescreen TV so that the images could be seen clearly by everyone. The Bailiff knew that sometime later that day, the DVD player and TV would be used by Daniel. Daniel then looked over the evidence table a little more closely to find that the prosecution had labeled the bullet found as their exhibit. To Daniel that didn't matter to him as much as the fact that the bullet had been found at all.

Bill Berman was seated at the defendant's table. Linda was organizing some last minute evidence that she was going to use as the prosecution. She put this new evidence on the evidence table and tossed Daniel a copy of the reports onto the top of his briefcase. As he looked over this stack of paperwork, the doors to the back of the courtroom opened.

Daniel turned around to see twelve prospective jurors being ushered into the jury box to his right by the jury coordinator. Daniel could see the jury coordinator marking up a large whiteboard with a marker of some kind. The jury coordinator then put the whiteboard on Judge Bishop's desktop. Daniel looked over the prospective jurors to see at least two familiar faces in the jury box.

He saw Miss Dwight from a recent case and Mr. Juan Rivera III. Daniel waved to them as he was touched on his right shoulder. Daniel turned around to find Nancy standing there. She handed him some paperwork, handed Linda a copy of the same paperwork and then abruptly left the courtroom.

Daniel looked over the paperwork which turned out to be the inventory of Mr. Quinest's motor vehicle. Daniel was mildly amused to see that the backseat had a homemade compartment under the seat to hide things inside. This compartment contained all sorts of climbing gear, clothes, a bloody sock and blood soaked boots.

The next sheets of paper were the lab results on the blood soaked sock and boots. The lab results indicated that the blood soaked sock had the victim's blood type on it, which was determined to be O positive. The blood soaked boots contained the same blood type found on the sock, but the lab found on the outside edge of the toe of the right boot, the blood was type B positive. Linda looked over at Daniel and the new evidence to the case shaking her head in disbelief as she tossed the paperwork into her open briefcase; Daniel turned to face Bill.

"Bill, by any chance do you know what your blood type is?"

"B positive; why?"

"No particular reason," replied Daniel as the left door to the front of the courtroom opened; the Bailiff stood up.

"All rise, criminal court for the 6th judicial district in the Town of Silverton in San Juan County, Colorado, is now in session. The Honorable Judge Larry Bishop, presiding, over case number 14CR299," he said.

Everyone stood up until Judge Bishop sat down at his bench.

"You may be seated. This is the trial phase of the *People V. Bill Berman,* case number 14CR299. A jury has been summoned for this case and has been seated in the jury box. There are twelve prospective jurors being nine primary and three alternates," said Larry as everyone sat down.

Larry put on his reading glasses and opened the case file that was sitting before him on his left. He briefly glanced over to his right to see the whiteboard before continuing his speech.

"Are there any members of the jury that do not reside in San Juan County?" asked Larry as he looked over at the jury box; no hands went up, so he continued with his speech.

"Are there any members of the jury that are not eighteen years of age?"

No hands went up, so he continued once again.

"Are there any members of the jury that cannot see or hear well enough to be a juror, or are there any members of the jury that cannot read, speak or write English?"

No hands went up, so he continued with his speech.

"Are there any members of the jury that have had prior jury duty service, meaning that you were selected as a juror for a criminal or civil trial in the past twelve months?"

One hand went up from juror number twenty-nine.

"Sir, you are juror number one in the front row. When was your jury service?"

"Four months ago in a civil trial in your courtroom, Your Honor," he said standing up.

"Very well, you are excused; see my clerk down the hall. Jury coordinator, move juror eleven to juror one's spot and call another juror to be an alternate."

"Yes, Your Honor. Juror number forty-one, please go to juror eleven's spot," she said.

The new prospective juror moved to the appropriate place.

"Juror eleven, having heard the questions earlier from being in the back of the courtroom, do you meet the requirements as I have set forth for jury duty?" asked Larry.

"Yes, Your Honor," he said.

"Are there any members of the jury that know any members of the parties or witnesses involved in this case?"

Two more hands went up. Larry looked down at his jury board.

"Juror number nine, who do you know?"

"The defense attorney; he defended me with Your Honor in a courthouse in Grand Junction," said Juan Rivera III, standing up.

"What is your name, sir?"

"Juan Rivera III, Your Honor."

"I thought I recognized you, sir. You're dismissed; see my clerk down the hall. Juror number twelve, please take his place and jury coordinator, please call another juror," said Larry.

"Yes, Your Honor. Juror number fifty, please take juror twelve's place," she said.

The juror stood up and took Juan's place; another took their place as an alternate.

"New juror number twelve, having heard the questions from the back of the courtroom, do you meet the requirements?"

"Yes, Your Honor, I do," she said.

"Juror number four, who do you know?"

"The defense attorney, Your Honor."

"What's your name?"

"Miss Ezra Dwight, Your Honor."

"Very well, you're dismissed. See my clerk down the hall. Juror number ten, take her place. Jury coordinator, call another juror."

"Yes, Your Honor. Juror number twenty-two, please take juror four's place."

"Yes, Your Honor."

The jurors moved around once again and finally Larry prepared to let the other prospective jurors go. Larry turned the courtroom over to the prosecution first. Daniel was going over some notes that he had taken. Linda stood up to address the court.

"Your Honor, the prosecution is satisfied with the jury that has been selected," she said as she sat back down.

"So noted. Defense counsel, are you satisfied with the jury?"

"I am, Your Honor depending on the answers from two questions from the jury," said Daniel, standing up.

"So noted. Does the prosecution have any objection to defense counsel's request?"

"None, Your Honor," said Linda standing up and sitting back down.

"So noted. You may ask your questions, defense counsel."

"Thank you, Your Honor. Ladies and gentlemen of the jury and alternate jurors, did any of you not graduate from high school?"

asked Daniel as he stood up; since no hands went up, Daniel went on to his next question.

"Do you believe that a person has the right to defend themselves if they are attacked?" asked Daniel as he watched all the heads nodding up and down in agreement. Daniel continued, "I'm satisfied with the jury that has been seated, Your Honor."

"So noted. Is the prosecution ready with their opening statements?"

"We are, Your Honor."

"Defense counsel, are you ready with your opening statements?"

"I am, Your Honor."

"So noted. The prosecution can begin with their opening statements after a short recess and the members of the jury that wish to take notes are issued pads of paper and pens or pencils. This court will recess for ten minutes," said Larry, banging down his gavel.

Larry simply stood up and walked out the left side of the courtroom. He had given the Bailiff a special hand signal not to announce anything. Ten minutes later, Larry returned. The jury returned, ready to take notes and Larry looked at the back of the courtroom.

"Ladies and gentlemen who are seated in the back of the courtroom, I thank you for showing up for potential jury service, but you are not needed. Please see my clerk down the hall. Prosecution, you may start with your opening statements," said Larry.

The prosecution opened up with their usual rhetoric about the defendant being a very bad person. She went on to say how cold and heartless the defendant was in not helping the deceased with the gunshot wound. After her very ugly opening statements, Daniel stood up to speak. He was stopped momentarily by Judge Bishop.

"Ladies and gentlemen of the jury and juror alternates, I have to instruct you that there is no affirmative defense to the charge of manslaughter," said Larry, looking at the jury box.

"Ladies and gentlemen of the jury, simply put, my client was in the wrong place at the wrong time; this is despite being a known fact that my client was required by his security company regulations to check on any alarms that could go off at his facility.

It is a sad fact my client, after being put into the wrong place at the wrong time, had to deal with something else more urgent."

Daniel stopped for a minute because some of the members of the jury were paying attention and were taking notes.

"This unfortunate misplacement was further aggravated by a set of unforgivable circumstances that were the direct result of the deceased. I will show you, ladies and gentlemen of the jury, that the deceased was directly responsible for his own demise."

Daniel stopped speaking once again.

"Contrary to popular belief of what you may see in the movies and on TV, I do not have to put my client on the stand and I have no intention of putting my client on the stand. Also, my esteemed colleague here is going to put me on the witness stand in an attempt to discredit me and my client. The only thing I think she will prove is something much to her own embarrassment."

Daniel stopped once again for the chuckling to stop before continuing.

"My client, just like you in a given set of circumstances, has the innate right of self-defense to protect himself, or herself, or others. I will show that the deceased had many opportunities to seek medical attention for his gunshot wound from many different sources. In fact, if the deceased had simply gone to the police to report this unfortunate gunshot wound, then this whole trial would never have had to happen."

He paused this time to watch the jury closely.

"I will show that the deceased maliciously attacked my client and the deceased showed total indifference towards my client in many ways. First, the deceased illegally entered the facility after being terminated. Second, when my client went to investigate the alarms that were going off in a restricted area, the deceased shot my client at least three times. These gunshots destroyed my client's uniform, bulletproof vest and radio to name a few things."

Daniel looked across the jury once again seeing many more taking notes this time.

"Third, after shooting my client, the deceased aggravated the situation by kicking my client in the left arm on the way out of the facility. The deceased never bothered to lend first aid, call for help for my client or do anything else to make sure that my client was assisted. I will prove this and many more things before this case is over; thank you," said Daniel, sitting back down at the defendant's table.

Daniel was sitting down for some time before Linda decided to call her first witness. The witness was the Silverton Town Marshal, Nancy Gills. She took the witness stand, was sworn in by the Bailiff and waited for the questions to start. Linda approached the witness stand.

"Will you please state your name and occupation for the court's records?" asked Linda, nicely.

"My name is Nancy Gills and I am currently serving the position of the Town Marshal for the Town of Silverton."

"Approximately how long have you been in that position?"

"Over ten years."

"Did someone summon you to the deceased's residence in April of this year?"

"Yes."

"Is that someone in this courtroom?"

"Yes, they both are."

"Would you please identify those people?"

"The defense attorney, seated at the defendant's table, and his private investigator, Jessica Kim, seated directly behind him."

"Let the court records show that the witness identified Attorney Daniel Marcos and his Private Investigator, Jessica Kim. Did the defense attorney say anything to you, during the phone call to your office that was not normal when summoning help?" Linda asked carefully choosing her words.

"Yes, he said that I should bring along the Silverton Town Medical Examiner, Bob Boyington and the San Juan County Coroner. At the time, the duty coroner was the Chief Coroner Nabiya Quartez."

"Did you think the defense attorney's request was normal?"

"Objection, Your Honor, calls for an opinion," said Daniel standing up and then sitting back down.

"Objection, sustained," said Larry.

"No further questions, Your Honor; your witness, defense counsel," said Linda as she sat down. Daniel stood up but did not approach the witness stand.

"I have no questions at this time, Your Honor, for the witness, but I reserve my right to recall this witness at a later date for questioning," said Daniel, sitting back down.

"So noted. The witness is excused. Prosecution, you may call your next witness," said Larry.

"Before I call my next witness, Your Honor, I would like to introduce prosecution exhibit one, the cell phone records of defense counsel on the day in question. Exhibit two, the phone records of the Silverton Town Marshal's office on the day in question. Exhibit three, the business cards of defense counsel's private investigator and Exhibit four, defense counsel's business card," she said handing Larry the evidence.

"Very well, you may call the witness," said Larry after the evidence was entered into the court records by the court clerk.

"The prosecution calls Attorney Daniel Marcos to the stand," she said.

Daniel stood up and walked over to the witness stand. He sat down in the chair in the witness stand after being sworn in by the Bailiff. Daniel made sure that he sat straight up in the chair and looked alternately between the jury and the prosecutor. He waited for the questions that were to come. To add to the tension in the courtroom about Daniel being on the stand, Linda walked deliberately over to the jury box.

"Ladies and gentlemen of the jury, I am not going to ask why Mr. Marcos was over at the deceased's residence. That question could possibly be construed as a violation of the attorney/client privilege. So, I will ask other questions of Mr. Marcos."

Linda walked over to the witness stand.

"Mr. Marcos, on the day you called Marshal Nancy Gills, what evidence did you have to support the request that she bring along the Silverton Town Medical Examiner, Bob Boyington and the San Juan County Coroner Nabiya Quartez?"

"First of all, I had no idea on the day in question that the duty San Juan County Coroner was going to be Nabiya Quartez. I surmised that due to the late hour of the day and the day of the week it was, the on-call coroner would be summoned."

"All right, so you didn't know who the duty coroner was; please continue."

"Myself and my associate, Jessica Kim, discovered three pieces of evidence that would lead a reasonable person, like members of the jury, to believe that a corpse or corpses were going to be found inside the residence."

"What was that evidence?" Again, Daniel could tell that Linda was carefully choosing the wording for her questions. She was uncomfortable with Daniel on the witness stand.

"First, myself and my associate discovered a stack of newspapers on the front porch; I counted nine of them. Second, I observed, through the windows in the front door, that there was a large stack of mail underneath the mail slot that was cut into the door. Third, my associate was scared by a large blowfly that hit the window she was looking into at the time."

"Seems reasonable to me, Your Honor; how would a large blowfly indicate a possible corpse or corpses?"

"It is a known fact, Your Honor and the jury, that insects like flies and mosquitoes are not active at this altitude until after Memorial Day weekend."

"Does your client or you, own a 10MM caliber, semi-automatic handgun?"

"Yes, I own a 10MM caliber, semi-automatic pistol and my client owns one and is issued one, for security duty use and another one he keeps by his bedside."

"Did you attend the death of the deceased?"

"No, I did not."

"Were you trying to conceal a death for your client perhaps then?"

"No, I was not trying to conceal a death. According to Colorado Revised Statutes, 18-8-109, that crime is a misdemeanor offense and I can be disbarred for such a blatant criminal action."

"Then may be you can tell this court how you were able to determine a date and time of death prior to the coroner's official report. This surmises you, once again, didn't attend the death of the deceased and then fail to report such to the authorities."

"Daniel, don't answer that question; I think she's trying to entrap you in my courtroom," said Larry as he glared at Linda.

"Thank you, Your Honor, for your concern, but I am well aware of my esteemed colleague's courtroom tactics in this respect. In fact, I would have been very worried if she had not tried something like this with me in court and under oath. I will answer the question, if Your Honor permits me," said Daniel.

Larry thought about it for a few minutes before answering.

"Very well, Daniel, you can answer the question, but remember, she is a prosecutor," said Larry.

"Thank you," replied Daniel as he repositioned himself in the witness chair. He cleared his throat, looked over at the jury and then into the spectator's area.

"I utilized two pieces of evidence that would lead a reasonable person, like the jury, to conclude a date and time of death."

"And what were those two pieces of evidence?"

"As I stated earlier, under oath to tell the truth, there was a stack of newspapers in front of the door to the residence. I merely looked over the dates on the newspapers and found the earliest date. There was also a stack of mail inside of the door, which blocked it from being opened."

"Sounds reasonable enough, but what if I had then decided to leave town without telling anyone?"

"I had considered that possibility, but if I was going to leave town that abruptly, I would have made sure that I placed either a stop mail notice in at the post office, forwarded my mail to where I was going to or had someone retrieve my mail until the forwarding took place."

"I might do the same thing; what about the newspapers and all of my personal effects?"

"I would have stopped the newspaper or cancelled my subscription telling the person I talked to that I had to leave town and would not be returning. My personal effects, minus those items that I need to use on a daily basis, would have been packed up and sent ahead to either a storage facility or to my new address."

"Okay, how, then, did you establish the time of death so accurately?"

"All of the clocks in the deceased's home, that I could see in the living room area, had all stopped at exactly the same time; 7:38 p.m."

A man in the front row of benches, in the fourth position in the spectator's area, gasped. Daniel heard this and leaned forward a little in his chair to get a better look at the person who made this noise. The man's eyes were wide-open along with his mouth. Daniel looked up at Judge Bishop.

"Your Honor, I believe my statement to this court has elicited a response from the spectator area," said Daniel pointing to the man.

"Sir, would you please stand up and tell the court your name?" asked Larry.

The man stood up from the fourth seat position in the front row of the spectator's area behind the prosecutor's table.

"My name is Joe Kapps, Your Honor. I was Mr. Quinest's coworker. In fact, my desk is directly opposite his in Lab Six."

"That's nice, Mr. Kapps, but do you have anything to add to Mr. Marcos' statement?" asked Larry, getting a little impatient.

"Yes, Your Honor, the clock on Mr. Quinest's desk stopped on the date and time Mr. Marcos stated. I have had our facility maintenance personnel change the battery in the clock several times, but it still doesn't work."

"Thank you, Mr. Kapps, you may be seated," said Larry as he turned to look at Linda.

"Is the prosecution satisfied with the honesty of the witness' statements that they have made in open court?" asked Larry.

"Yes, Your Honor, the prosecution is satisfied with the validity of the statements. The prosecution has no further questions for this witness," she said as she sat down at her table.

"The witness is excused," said Larry.

"Thank you, Your Honor," said Daniel as he took his seat at his desk.

"The prosecution may call its next witness," said Larry, looking at Linda.

"Thank you, Your Honor. The prosecution calls Bob Boyington to the stand."

Bob stood up, walked towards and took his seat in the witness stand. After Sergio swore him in, Linda walked up and started her questioning.

"Would you please state, for the court's records, your name and occupation?"

"My name is Bob Boyington and I am currently serving the position of the Silverton Town Medical Examiner."

"And how long have you been in that position?"

"Almost twenty years."

"Were you summoned to the residence of one Bob Quinest early this year?"

"Yes."

"Is the party, or parties, who summoned you to the residence, present in this courtroom?"

"Yes, they are both present."

"Would you point them out to the jury?"

"Nancy Gills and Mr. Marcos," he said pointing at both of them.

"Let the court's records show that the witness identified Attorney Daniel Marcos once again. Did you find a dead body within the residence once Nancy Gills and you gained entry?"

"Yes."

"No further questions, Your Honor; your witness Mr. Marcos," said Linda as she took her seat at her table.

Daniel stood up and walked over to the witness stand.

"Mr. Boyington, just two questions. First, how did you know that the occupant, or occupants, of the residence were deceased?"

"Simple, Mr. Marcos, there was the unmistakable foul stench of rotting flesh that filled my nose when Nancy and I gained access to the residence. I then stumbled through the residence to discover Mr. Quinest's bloated body in the bedroom."

"Good answer, sir. My second question is, do you have to have any medical training or even first aid training to be designated the medical examiner for a town in the State of Colorado?"

"Objection, Your Honor, irrelevant and immaterial," snapped Linda.

"Your Honor, my question is very relevant and very material to my client's defense," said Daniel, quickly thinking while in open court.

"Objection overruled this time. The witness will answer the question," said Larry as he looked at the jury instead of the witness.

"No, Mr. Marcos, the State of Colorado does not require any type of medical training nor does the State of Colorado require even first aid training to be designated the medical examiner. My only job as a town medical examiner is to pronounce someone dead so that the respective county coroner can begin the autopsy."

"Thank you, Mr. Boyington. I have no more questions of this witness."

"The witness is excused and this court is in recess until 1:00 p.m.," said Larry, banging his gavel down and standing up.

"All rise," said Sergio as everyone left the courtroom for lunch.

CHAPTER 8

After the lunch recess, everyone was seated back in the courtroom. Sergio stood up as well as the rest of the courtroom. Larry entered the courtroom and walked up the three steps to his bench. He then sat down in his chair at the bench.

"All rise," said Sergio.

"You may be seated," said Larry as he put on his reading glasses and opened the case file back up.

Everyone sat down and remained silent before Larry spoke again.

"Is the prosecution ready to call its next witness?"

"We are, Your Honor. The prosecution calls Nabiya Quartez to the stand."

Nabiya took her seat in the witness stand. After being sworn in by Sergio, Linda approached the witness stand. Daniel stood up so that he could address the court.

"Your Honor, this witness is potentially hostile to the defense," said Daniel as he remained standing.

"In what way, Mr. Marcos?" asked Larry.

"The witness, because I interrupted her dinner, threatened to have me arrested and charged with false reporting to authorities."

"Very well, the court will take your objection under advisement," said Larry as Daniel sat down.

"Would you state for the court records, your name and occupation?" asked Linda.

"My name is Nabiya Quartez. I am currently serving the position of the San Juan County Chief Coroner in the State of Colorado," said Nabiya while looking straight past Linda to Daniel.

"How long have you had this position?"

"Almost fifteen years."

"On the date in question, as established earlier in this case, were you summoned to the residence of one Bob Quinest?"

"Yes."

"Is the person, or persons, who summoned you to the deceased's residence present in this courtroom?"

"Only one of the two persons who summoned me to the residence is present."

"Can you point to that person, who is present, in the courtroom?"

"The defense counsel, Daniel Marcos," said Nabiya pointing her left index finger at Daniel. Daniel seemed unconcerned at this point.

"Let the court records show that the witness identified the defense counsel Daniel Marcos. Do you know who the absent party is who summoned you to the deceased's residence?"

"Yes, the other party who summoned me to the deceased's residence is the Silverton Town Medical Examiner Bob Boyington."

"Did you, or someone in your office, find a cause of death for Mr. Quinest?"

"Not directly; one of my duty coroners was able to determine the cause of death."

"Is the person in your office who determined the cause of death available for questioning?"

"Probably not, since this person works the nightshift and is more than likely sleeping."

"No further questions, Your Honor."

Linda sat down at her table as Daniel stood up from his.

"Miss Quartez, did I assist you with the deceased?"

"Yes, Mr. Marcos you did assist me with the deceased. You brought the gurney from the back of my official car up the stairs and into the deceased's residence."

"For the sake of argument and if it pleases both the court and my esteemed colleague, I will allow Miss Quartez here to read the cause of death from the official report. I figure, Your Honor, that any of the assistant coroners are just as competent and qualified as the chief coroner," said Daniel.

"Does the prosecution have any objections?" asked Larry.

"None, Your Honor," said Linda, standing up, smiling and then sitting back down.

"Please read into the court records the official cause of death," said Daniel.

"The probable cause of death is from the complications of an untreated gunshot wound to the right ankle. There were multiple, small bone fragments in the wound as well as red streaks radiating out from the wound. There was also the presence of a foul odor that is associated with rotting flesh. Lab test results indicated gangrene infection was present along with more small, bone fragments in the sample sent to the lab for testing."

"Just a few more questions for you, Miss Quartez; how was it determined that the wound was, in fact, a gunshot wound?"

"A nitrite test was conducted on the wound which showed positive for gunshot residue known as cordite. The entrance hole was measured at .400 inches in diameter and there was an exit hole."

"Was there, to the best of your knowledge, a bullet found?"

"No, not to the best of my knowledge, no bullet was found."

"Do you happen to know the deceased's blood type?"

"One moment," said Nabiya as she looked through the top portion of the report before continuing, "the deceased's blood type is O+."

"Could this gunshot wound have been self-inflicted?"

"The wound could have been self-inflicted, but it is unlikely, unless you're a sadist."

"Why not? By self-inflicting the gunshot wound, with the same caliber weapon my client owns, and then not seeking medical treatment for the wound, would be the perfect way to frame my client; corpses can't talk."

"Objection, Your Honor, calls for speculation and opinion," said Linda.

"Your Honor, think about it for a minute. A self-inflicted gunshot wound, which I would intentionally not seek medical treatment for, would be a perfect way to frame my client. As long as the bullet is from my client's duty issue weapon, in this case a 10MM semi-automatic handgun, the coroner, the ballistics technician and the D.A. would all reach the wrong conclusion."

Daniel paused for a few seconds before continuing.

"Everyone would wrongly conclude that my client not only committed the crime, but then some how coerced the deceased into intentionally not seeking medical attention for the gunshot wound."

"Prosecution, can you disprove any of defense counsel's statements?" asked Larry, looking rather harshly at the prosecution for missing something so obvious.

"No, Your Honor, I cannot disprove any of those statements."

"Objection overruled, the witness will answer the question."

"I have no answer to the question, Your Honor."

"I have no further questions, Your Honor," said Daniel, sitting down at his table.

"Does the prosecution wish to redirect?"

"No, Your Honor."

"The witness is excused. The prosecution can call its next witness."

"The prosecution calls Mr. Garth Smith to the witness stand," said Linda, loudly.

The Colorado Bureau of Investigation's newest Senior Ballistics Technician took the witness stand. After he was sworn in by Sergio, Linda picked up an evidence bag from the evidence table. She then handed it to Mr. Smith.

"Would you please state, for the court records, your name and occupation," said Linda.

"My name is Garth Smith and I am now the senior ballistics technician at the Colorado Bureau of Investigation effective this morning."

"How long have you been in that position?"

"Seventeen years, five months and twelve days."

"Calling your attention to prosecution exhibit C, would you please state what the evidence is?"

"The item you handed me is labeled as an evidence bag," he said, flatly.

The whole courtroom started laughing; Larry banged his gavel down several times to quiet the laughter.

"Quiet in my courtroom!" he yelled and the courtroom went back to being quiet.

"Your Honor, could I rephrase the question?" asked Linda, after she realized what mistake she had made.

"You may proceed as long as defense counsel has no objections?" asked Larry as he looked at Daniel.

"No objections, Your Honor," said Daniel, standing up, smiling and then sitting back down.

"Do you recognize the contents of the evidence bag?" she asked.

"Yes, the contents of the evidence bag appear to be a badly damaged bullet."

"Did you, or someone on your staff, examine that badly damaged bullet?"

"Yes, I examined the bullet after it was sent to me by the San Juan County Sheriff's Department, I believe."

"Can you tell this court what your findings were?"

"No, I cannot tell this court what my findings were."

"Why?"

"I was not expecting to be in court today, so I didn't bring my notepad with me. I was also not expecting to find my teacher and mentor slumped over the wheel of his car in the bureau's parking lot. I am also keenly aware that defense counsel doesn't like witnesses quoting their notes from memory."

"Your Honor, that statement sounds like Intimidating a Witness or Victim to me. I request that this court hold defense counsel accountable for such a crime," said Linda as Daniel stood up to address the court.

"Your Honor, if it pleases the court and my esteemed colleague, I am not intimidating the witness or victim in this case. As a criminal defense attorney, I am aware that such a crime is punishable by disbarment and a minimum four year prison term for the felony offense. Mr. Smith has been in court with me before on several occasions and is keenly aware of my thoroughness in questioning a witness on the stand," said Daniel as he remained standing.

Larry turned to face the witness.

"Is what defense counsel says true, sir?" asked Larry.

"It is, Your Honor; I am very well aware of defense counsel's thoroughness."

"Very well, does the prosecution still feel that defense counsel should be arrested and charged with violating Colorado Revised Statutes Title 18, Article 8, Part 704? I believe that there is a difference between being thorough and being a criminal?"

"I will withdraw my statement for wanting defense counsel arrested and charged with violating C.R.S. 18-8-704."

"Is that apology acceptable to you defense counsel?" asked Larry, nicely.

"Apology accepted, Your Honor," he replied, sitting back down.

"Here's a copy of your ballistics report, Mr. Smith. Can you tell this court if you were able to tell caliber and distinctive marks on this bullet?" asked Linda as she handed him his ballistics report.

Mr. Smith cleared his throat before speaking as he took the report into his left hand.

"The bullet was badly damaged after having passed through a body part of unknown origin and penetrated a piece of sheet metal. The bullet's weight is approximately 589 grains and its base measurement is approximately .400 inches in diameter."

"Please continue to read the report findings," said Linda as if to urge him on.

"This base measurement would seem to indicate, although not conclusively, that the weapon which fired the bullet would have been a .400 Corbon®, .40 Smith and Wesson, 10MM Automatic or a .40 Super."

"Did you or someone on your staff find any indentifying marks?"

"Yes, I did find some indentifying marks as you refer to them."

"Would you please tell this court what you or someone on your staff found?"

Mr. Smith looked over at Daniel for just a few seconds before he answered.

"The bullet, after having been thoroughly examined under a microscope at the lab was found to have small fragments of sheet metal, cloth, blood and bone fragments on the inside and outside of the bullet. The inside peg of the bullet had dried blood and bone."

"Is there anything more about the examination you performed that you would like to tell this court?"

"Yes, all of these items were found on the peeled back edges of the bullet, the peg in the middle of the bullet and the base of the bullet."

"Can you tell this court if you know what type of bone and blood was found?"

"A chemical analysis of the bone fragments indicated that they were human in origin. The blood found was determined to be human in origin as well."

"What blood type was the blood?"

"O+, same as the deceased's."

"No further questions, Your Honor; your witness, defense," said Linda with a smirk on her face.

"Thank you, Linda. Mr. Smith, my sincere condolences on your recent loss. I can empathize with you on having lost a teacher and mentor. I have lost a few in my time as well. I surmise that when you found him, he had been deceased for some length of time?"

"Yes, Mr. Marcos, he had been dead a couple of hours according to the Denver County Coroner's office."

"Your Honor, is defense counsel ever going to ask a question of this witness?" she asked, loudly.

"I am, Your Honor. I was merely showing some empathy towards the witness; he's had a long day already. Mr. Smith, I will keep my questions simple."

"Thank you, Mr. Marcos."

"Recalling your attention to your ballistics report and prosecution Exhibit C, is it possible that the bullet may in fact be a 10MM Automatic round, such as the one issued to my client for duty use?"

"Yes, it is quite possible."

"Is it also possible that this bullet is in fact a 180-grain, Federal, Hydrashock® round?"

"It is highly possible, Mr. Marcos. The bullet has a peg in the middle of it that is a signature of the said personal defense round. The bullet's edges peel back, like that bullet's did upon impact with something like human flesh, or any hard object like sheet metal or armor plating."

"I surmise, then, that the lab test you ran on the dried blood on the bullet was the Luminol® test to determine if the blood was animal or human?"

"Yes, that's correct, the test results indicated positive for human."

"Thank you, Mr. Smith; no further questions for the witness," said Daniel as he sat back down at his table.

"The witness is excused," said Larry.

"Your Honor, the prosecution rests," said Linda.

"So noted, is the defense ready to put on its part of the case?" asked Larry.

"We are, Your Honor," said Daniel.

"Very well, this court will recess for lunch. This court will reconvene at 1:30 p.m., " said Larry, banging down his gavel and standing up.

"All rise," said Sergio.

At 1:30 p.m., everyone was back in the courtroom. After Judge Bishop had sat down at his bench, Daniel was ready to put on his first witness, Barry Goldman. Daniel stood up, taking his legal pad with him towards the witness stand. Larry put on his reading glasses and looked at Daniel.

"You may put on your first witness, Mr. Marcos," said Larry.

"Thank you, Your Honor. The defense calls Barry Goldman to the stand. Your Honor, may I have some time for my secretary to set up the court's DVD player for presenting evidence?"

"So long as the prosecution has no objections, your secretary can set up the DVD player."

"I have registered my objections to this court in accordance with Rule 41, Colorado Revised Statutes, on defense video and audio exhibits A, B, C and D."

"This court has noted the objection prior to this trial. However, this court would be remiss in its duty not to allow the defense exhibits entered into the record and give the prosecution a chance to disprove defense's evidence by cross-examination of witnesses. This court has a duty to the defendant to protect their Sixth Amendment right."

"Thank you, Your Honor; are you satisfied, Miss Prosecutor?" asked Daniel, glaring at her.

"The prosecution is satisfied, Your Honor."

"The defense may proceed, now that the witness has been sworn in and the DVD player has been set up."

"Thank you, Your Honor. The witness has been previously sworn in by the prosecution. To save time in court, I have only a few questions of this witness."

"Proceed, Mr. Marcos."

"Mr. Goldman, does your company provide the physical security, which includes video and audio surveillance devices at a place called the Baltimore Testing Center?"

"Yes."

"Is my client an employee of your company?"

"Yes."

Daniel looked down at his notepad before he asked the next set of questions.

"Does your company employ my client in a capacity to possibly use deadly force?"

"Yes, your client is authorized to use deadly force in any number of situations due to certain circumstances of the facility."

"Are there any signs at your facility that states deadly force could be used against unauthorized personnel?"

"Yes, there are three such signs. One at the entrance, one outside lab three and one outside of lab six."

"Could someone break into your facility?"

"Objection, Your Honor, calls for speculation or opinion," said Linda.

"Your Honor, I simply want to prove two points. Point one being that no place is completely secure and the second point is, the deceased did in fact break into the facility; was armed and shot my client," replied Daniel.

"Your Honor, defense counsel cannot prove any of this," said Linda, again, loudly.

"I can prove it, Your Honor. If nothing else, I can prove motive by the deceased for breaking into the facility and committing industrial espionage."

"Oh, please, Your Honor, defense counsel cannot prove any of his statements," said Linda, marching up to the bench.

"Your Honor, I can prove all of this with the witness. All of my evidence was gathered legally and entered into this court's records in accordance with Rule 41 of Colorado Revised Statutes. I am aware of prosecution's objections to some of my evidence, she has challenged me in open court and I deserve the right to respond."

"I agree with defense counsel. Does the prosecution disagree?" asked Larry.

"No objections, Your Honor," replied Linda as she sat back down at her table.

"Thank you, Your Honor."

"The objection is overruled and the witness will answer the question pending defense counsel's proof statement."

"Go ahead, Mr. Goldman, answer the question," said Daniel.

"Yes, it is possible to break into the facility, especially at night or during bad weather conditions."

"Thank you, Mr. Goldman. Without giving away any secrets, what does the Boston Testing Center do?"

"Objection, Your Honor, where is defense counsel going with this line of questioning?" barked Linda.

"Your Honor, I'm about to prove industrial espionage."

"Objection overruled, the witness will answer."

"The Boston Testing Center is a US government defense research development and testing facility. We have a contract with the Defense Advanced Research Projects Agency or DARPA as they are called."

Daniel looked down at his legal pad, flipped through a few pages and then looked back up at Barry.

"Was the deceased ever employed by the Boston Testing Center?"

"Yes, the deceased worked in lab six, which is a think tank of sorts for DARPA."

"So, the deceased had ideas, drawings, blueprints, etc., but they weren't really his, were they?"

"No, the ideas, etc., are company property and are not theirs."

"Now, on the night my client was shot by the deceased, was my client on shift and armed?"

"Yes, your client was on shift the night he was shot, which was the same night the deceased's employment was terminated."

"There, Your Honor, I just proved some of my motive statement about the deceased and I will show more evidence of this," said Daniel smiling.

"Any objections, prosecution?" asked Larry.

"None so far, Your Honor," replied Linda, quietly.

"Did any of the computers, even those belonging to the deceased, have anything on them related to the deceased?"

"Yes, there were two files on the deceased's computer, that were copied onto a CD or maybe more than one CD while the alarm system was going off on the night your client was shot."

"Were those two files projects that the deceased created?"

"Yes, they were. One file we suspect ended up going to Boeing and the other one we have no clue."

"There, Your Honor, I just proved the industrial espionage part of my statement."

"So you did; please continue," said Larry.

"Now, how many labs does the facility have?"

"Six total, Mr. Marcos."

"Did any of the labs conduct, store or allow hazardous materials or operations?"

"Yes, labs three and five."

"Your Honor, I will read a short statement about those labs. Lab three conducts destructive testing on materials sent in for testing. There are rockets and grenades and machine guns, explosives and landmines, to name a few items. Lab five is a shooting range for rifles, shotguns and handguns."

Daniel flipped through his legal pad again before continuing.

"Can employees of the Baltimore Testing Center use lab five?"

"Yes, that is where I requalify my armed security personnel every quarter."

"Besides labs three and five, are there other weapons at the facility?"

"Yes, I conceal carry along with the CEO, CIO, COO and CFO. I think there are about fifty other employees, all on different shifts and in different departments, that conceal carry. My security officers are armed, then there are four semi-automatic rifles and four semi-automatic shotguns in the guard shack. Each of those have two hundred rounds for the rifles and two hundred-fifty rounds of double-aught buckshot and slugs for the shotguns."

"What is my client's duty weapon?"

"A Glock® Model 20 with night sights, three 17-round magazines and 180 grain Hydra Shock™ rounds for personal defense; also, other uniform items."

"What caliber is the Glock® Model 20?"

"10 mm automatic."

"Your Honor, I would like to question this witness further, but it appears that you have given me the time-is-up signal."

"That is right, Mr. Marcos. This court is in recess until 7:30 a.m. tomorrow morning."

"All rise," said Sergio.

Everyone stood up and left the courtroom and Larry left the bench. Daniel drove to his place where he found Melanie's three kids on his front porch. He stepped out of his car and walked up to them; David spoke first.

"Our mom was taken to Denver by those FBI guys. She told us to come here."

"Good choice your mother made; won't you come inside, boys?" said Daniel, unlocking the door and opening it.

David, Seth and Todd all entered into Daniel's home. David went on the attack against Daniel after dinner.

"How come you're not in Denver with mom?"

"She is going to appear before what is called a Grand Jury. Do you take any American government or civics classes?"

"No."

"Well, simply put, the grand jury is the only place, as the defense attorney, I cannot go. Your mother has to stand alone; now, you need to go to bed."

Daniel knew it was going to be a very long night.

CHAPTER 9

Daniel was in court by 7:15 a.m. As he sorted through his notes that Lynn had taken during yesterday's testimony, Lynn was busy checking the DVD player to make sure that it was working properly. She returned to the table as Daniel was drinking his coffee.

"Good morning, Daniel," said Lynn.

"Good morning, Lynn. Please charge our client, Melanie Thompson, for another ten hours of work under the title of babysitting services."

"Okay."

A few minutes later Linda walked into the courtroom. She sat down at her table and opened up her briefcase. She took out her notepads from yesterday, looked over at Daniel and smiled. The Bailiff stood up to address the court. Larry was standing in the doorway to the courtroom.

"All rise, criminal court for the town of Silverton in San Juan County, Colorado, in the 6th judicial district, is now in session. The Honorable Judge Larry Bridget Bishop, presiding."

Larry walked up a few steps to his bench and opened up the case file.

"You may be seated. As I recall, Mr. Goldman was on the witness stand yesterday. The witness is to retake the stand," said Larry, putting on his reading glasses.

Barry walked up to the witness stand and sat down in the chair. Judge Bishop turned to face him.

"The witness is reminded that the oath they took yesterday applies today. Do you understand this order?" asked Larry.

"I do, Your Honor."

"Very well, the defense can continue its examination of the witness."

"Your Honor, the prosecution objects to the presentation of defense exhibits A through D, on the basis of violating Rule 41 Colorado Revised Statutes," said Linda.

"The objection is so noted, prosecution. This court will wait to rule on your objection until each piece of evidence is admitted into the court records. If the evidence presented has no bearing on the witness or witnesses for the defense, then I will rule for sustain on your objection for that piece of evidence."

"Thank you, Your Honor."

"Defense counsel, you may proceed."

"Thank you, Your Honor. Mr. Goldman, would you please tell the court, what we are about to watch?" said Daniel, pressing play on the DVD player.

The jury as well as the spectators all watched as a dark colored object ran from the main gate to the trash cans. The camera followed the object the entire time.

"That is a piece of my security surveillance system. That is camera 30 and it has both an infrared and a motion grid built into the camera's front lens."

"Meaning, either a heat source or source of motion would trigger the security surveillance system to follow the movement, even if it was the deceased?"

"Objection, Your Honor, calls for speculation or opinion."

"Not opinion or speculation, Your Honor; fact."

"I surmise that defense counsel can prove this?" asked Larry.

"Of course, Your Honor, I have three witnesses that can back up this statement."

"Proceed, defense counsel."

"Mr. Goldman, how are the trash cans picked up and dumped at your facility?"

"With a pair of large, mechanical arms."

"So, no one touches the trash cans?"

"Yes, that is correct."

"Thank you, Mr. Goldman. The witness is excused so that the defense may call Ms. Jessica Kim to the stand, unless my esteemed colleague has questions of this witness?"

"I have only one question, Your Honor. Mr. Goldman, could the dark object moving about be a bear or an elk or something of that nature?" asked Linda.

"It could be a wolverine, but not an elk or a bear."

"Why not?" asked Linda, looking for more ways to discredit the defense.

"I checked with the Colorado Division of Wildlife and found out bears are not active at that altitude until late May. The elk are in New Mexico until mid-May."

"No further questions, Your Honor."

"The witness is excused."

Jessica Kim replaced Mr. Goldman on the witness stand. After she was sworn in, Daniel started asking her questions.

"Your Honor, in the interest of speeding up this trial and if my esteemed colleague has no objections, I am not going to ask Miss Kim about her background. Your Honor and my esteemed colleague are well aware of her background."

"Indeed we are aware of her background, counselor. Does the prosecution object or stipulate to defense counsel's request?" asked Larry.

"The prosecution will stipulate."

"You may proceed, counselor, with your questioning."

"Thank you, Your Honor."

Daniel turned to face Jessica.

"Did you have an occasion to check those trash cans that were in the surveillance video we all watched, for fingerprints?" asked Daniel.

"I did and I found fresh prints on the back side of the far trash can. Those prints were then lifted and turned over to law enforcement officials for a positive identification."

"No further questions for this witness. At this time, I would like defense exhibit B to be entered into the court records."

Linda stood up from her table and walked towards the witness stand.

"Miss Kim, how long do fingerprints last in the outdoors?" asked Linda.

"In the State of Colorado, not longer than forty days."

"No further questions, Your Honor."

"The witness is excused. You may call your next witness, defense."

"The defense calls Marshal Nancy Gills to the stand."

Nancy walked up to the witness stand and sat down in the chair.

"Marshal Gills, were you given a set of fingerprints by my private investigator to determine who they belong to?"

"Yes, your private investigator turned over a set of fingerprints to me for a positive identification."

"Did you find out whose fingerprints they were?"

"Yes, my Automated Fingerprint Identification System or AFIS said that the fingerprints belonged to the deceased. The prints matched the left hand of the deceased from his Department of Defense fingerprint card."

"Thank you, Marshal Gills, no further questions for the witness."

Linda stood up from her table.

"The prosecution has no questions for this witness."

"The witness is excused. You may call your next witness defense."

"The defense calls Trooper Davis to the stand."

The trooper was sworn and waited for the questioning to begin. Daniel walked up to the witness stand.

"Trooper Davis, you have been in court with me a few times, so I won't ask you about your background. As long as the prosecution has no objections?" asked Daniel.

"No objections, Your Honor, the prosecution will stipulate to Trooper Davis' background," said Linda.

"Trooper Davis, before I start, I would like defense exhibits C and D entered into the court records."

"Very well," said Larry.

"Trooper Davis, would you please read the highlighted section of your own police report, which is labeled defense exhibit C, from the night my client was attacked?"

"A car came out of the facility at what appeared to be a high rate of speed, almost running me over. I could not get a license plate number or even see the driver very well."

"Would you be able to recognize this car if you saw it again?"

"Yes."

"Defense exhibit D is a picture of the deceased's car. Is that the car you saw that night?" asked Daniel, handing the trooper the picture of the car.

"Yes, that is the car, Mr. Marcos."

"Let the court records show that the witness identified the deceased's car."

"No questions for the witness, Your Honor," said Linda.

"The witness is excused. You may call your next witness."

"Thank you, Your Honor. Now, I'm about to prove that the deceased broke into the facility and shot my client."

"Which you may do, counselor, following our mid-morning recess."

"All rise," said Sergio as Judge Larry Bishop left the courtroom.

Twenty minutes later, the court reconvened. Daniel stood up and addressed the court, legal notepad in hand.

"Your Honor, the defense wishes to recall Marshal Gills to the stand," said Daniel.

"Objection, Your Honor; hasn't defense counsel already examined this witness?" protested Linda as she stood up.

"I have examined this witness before; however, this witness is part of both the prosecution's case and the defense's case. Therefore, I respectfully request to examine this witness on their knowledge of the deceased being on the property to commit several crimes."

"Prosecution still objects; the defense has no proof of his statement."

"Your Honor, then maybe the prosecution has no objection to the due process clauses of the Colorado State Constitution or the federal US Constitution?"

"The prosecution has no objections to the due process claim of the defense counsel on behalf of the client. Prosecution objects to defense counsel examining the witness again after they have been cross examined by me."

"Your Honor, Marshal Gills will prove the rest of my opening statements with proof positive that the deceased was on the property the night my client was attacked."

"Prosecution's objection is so noted. However, since the witness has further testimony relevant to the case, objection overruled. On the objection to defense exhibits A through D, the defense showed their relevancy to this case. The Rule 41 objection is, therefore, overruled."

"Thank you, Your Honor. Marshal Gills, will you retake the stand?"

Marshal Gills took her seat on the witness stand. Daniel approached her with his notepad of questions.

"Marshal Gills, is it customary for a deceased persons' effects to be inventoried by law enforcement personnel?"

"Yes, when there is abandoned property found by law enforcement or if the deceased has no immediate kin to claim the property."

"Do you need a search or seizure warrant to do this inventory?"

"No, an inventory search and inevitable discovery are some of the exceptions to obtaining a search or seizure warrant."

"Thank you, Marshal Gills."

Daniel walked over to the evidence table and picked up the next defense exhibit E. He walked over to the witness stand and handed Marshal Gills her copy of the inventory list.

"At this time, Your Honor, I would like defense exhibit E to be entered into evidence. The exhibit is an inventory list compiled by Marshal Gills of the deceased's motor vehicle."

"Prosecution has no objections, Your Honor."

"So noted. Defense exhibit E is entered into the court records."

"Marshal Gills, would you please read to the court the highlighted sections of the inventory of the deceased's motor vehicle?"

"Yes, the backseat was found to contain a hidden compartment under the seat. Inside this compartment I found climbing gear, a blood soaked shoe and blood soaked socks."

"Thank you, Marshal Gills. Can you tell this court if you had a lab identify the blood soaked shoe and determine if it was the deceased's or my client's blood type?"

"The lab confirmed both blood types were present, Mr. Marcos."

"Really? Both my client's and the deceased's? Could the lab tell you when the blood was put into or on the shoes?"

"The lab stated to me that the blood soaked shoe had the deceased's blood type inside and a bullet hole through the ankle portion of the shoe. The front tip of the same shoe contained your client's blood type."

Daniel walked over to the evidence table and picked up the blood soaked shoe.

"Your Honor, the defense would like to enter into evidence, defense exhibits F and G. The blood soaked shoe and the climbing gear."

"Prosecution has no objections."

"So noted. Defense exhibits F and G are entered into evidence."

"Marshal Gills, did you find any firearms while inventorying the deceased's personal property?"

"Yes, I found a rifle, shotgun and two handguns."

"What were the calibers of the handguns that you found?"

"The first one I found was a Smith & Wesson Model 1006 semi-automatic pistol. The other was a .25 caliber semi-automatic pistol of unknown make."

"Thank you, Marshal Gills. One more question, did you find anything else during the inventory that was not normal?"

"Objection, calls for opinion and speculation."

"Objection is overruled. The witness will answer the question."

"I found a large briefcase filled with $650,000 in cash in used $50's and $100's."

"No further questions, Your Honor."

"The prosecution has no questions for the witness."

"Very well, defense may call its next witness after the lunch break. Court will reconvene at 1:00 p.m."

"All rise," said Sergio.

Everyone left the courtroom. Daniel went home for lunch and returned by 12:45 p.m. As he was sitting down at his table, Lynn rushed in with some paperwork. She handed Daniel a writ of habeas corpus and a pen.

"Daniel, quickly sign this writ. I had to run up the stairs and down the back hallway before Linda arrived."

"Okay, who's this writ for?" asked Daniel, signing it and handing it back to Lynn.

"Our client, Melanie Thompson. Linda just had her arrested a few minutes ago."

"What is Linda going to charge her with?"

"Murder and theft."

Linda entered the courtroom. As she sat down, she opened up her briefcase and smiled.

"Have you interrogated my client without my presence?" asked Daniel.

"If you're referring to Melanie Thompson, she refuses to talk to me without your presence."

"I trained her well. Now, here's your copy of the writ of habeas corpus," said Daniel, handing her the second copy.

"Thank you, counselor. She's being held at the Ironton Town Marshal's office."

"I want a copy of the coroner's report when it is available."

"Certainly, counselor."

Sergio stood up as did the rest of the court. As Judge Bishop opened the door, he looked over his courtroom.

"All rise, criminal court for the Town of Silverton in San Juan County in the State of Colorado's 6th judicial district is now in session. The Honorable Judge Larry Bishop, presiding."

Larry walked up the steps to his bench and put on his reading glasses before addressing the court.

"You may be seated. During the lunch recess, the jury foreman handed me a slip of paper with a question on it for the defense counsel. Normally, I don't allow such things in my courtroom; Judge Kyle Tillman allows them. However, after reviewing the question, I am curious to the answer as well."

Judge Bishop paused before continuing.

"Does either defense counsel or prosecution have any objections to the jury asking a question?"

"No objections, Your Honor," said Linda.

"No objections, Your Honor," said Daniel.

"Very well, the question reads as follows. Do you, defense counsel, believe that the deceased broke into the facility, allegedly hurt your client for the purpose of committing industrial espionage?"

"Yes, I do believe that was the intent of the deceased."

"Thank you, counselor. You may call your next witness."

"Thank you, Your Honor. The defense calls Jessica Kim to the stand."

"Your Honor, the prosecution objects to this witness being recalled."

"Your Honor, my esteemed colleague has forced me to recall this witness because of the way she called the evidence and witnesses."

"Objection is overruled."

Jessica walked up to the witness stand as Daniel walked over to the evidence table. He picked up defense exhibit H which was an envelope containing the pictures she took. He walked over to the witness stand.

"The witness is reminded that they are still under oath," said Larry.

"Yes, Your Honor, I understand."

Daniel conversed with Lynn as Lynn started taking the pictures from the envelope and putting them up on the whiteboard in order.

"At this time, Your Honor, I would like to enter into evidence defense exhibits H-1 through H-38."

"Prosecution has no objection, Your Honor."

"So noted. The evidence shall be entered into the court records."

"Miss Kim, what are we, as the court, looking at?" asked Daniel.

"Those are infrared pictures taken by me using my camera that was equipped with a zero to 120 mm zoom lens. The place those pictures were taken was at the Baltimore Testing Center's employee elevator."

"When did you take these pictures?" asked Daniel.

"At night, a few months ago."

"What were you looking for, exactly?"

"You had asked me, via your replacement attorney Dale Lutezenberg, to look for dried blood that could be photographed as evidence. This photo evidence was proof the deceased was present at the facility."

"Are those white objects, in the photos, the dried blood that you were to be looking for?"

"Yes."

"No further questions, Your Honor."

Daniel sat down at his table as Linda stood up from hers.

"Miss Kim, how do we, as the court, know that those white objects are blood?" asked Linda.

"I had to use a special chemical that shows up dried blood under infrared light. The chemical reacts only with blood."

"Does this chemical react with human or animal blood?"

"The chemical reacts only with human blood. There is another chemical that reacts only with animal blood; I do not possess such an item."

"Where exactly did you find this blood?"

"On the floor of the employee elevator, up the walls of the elevator and on top of the emergency escape hatch. I found a large pool of blood on the top of the elevator which I sent a small sample to the lab for identification."

"Did you find blood anywhere else?"

"Yes, I found blood at the top of the elevator shaft, in the pit sword room of the elevator, in the maintenance shop for the elevator and at the exit to the maintenance shop."

"Do you know the results of this lab-tested sample?"

"No, I don't know of the results. I suspect that Marshal Gills may know."

"I also know the results of the lab tests. The blood type is the same as the deceased's; no further questions."

"Very well, the witness is excused," said Larry.

"The prosecution rests; we have no closing arguments."

"So noted; defense counsel?"

"The defense rests at this time, we also have no closing arguments."

"So noted. The jury will begin deliberations."

The court closed without a verdict. Daniel returned home to find Melanie's kids on the doorstep. He fixed them dinner and put them to bed. Once they were in bed, Daniel went to the Ironton Town Marshal's office to see Melanie.

CHAPTER 10

Julie looked up from her desk as Daniel entered her office. She smiled, stood up and greeted Daniel. He looked up at her and smiled, though he was very tired. He then yawned and stretched a little.

"Good evening counselor," said Julie, looking up at the clock behind him; 11:05 p.m.

"I wish to see my client, Melanie Thompson."

"Its late, counselor and I've already put the prisoners to bed. Besides, don't you think, at 11:05 p.m., you could keep normal hours?"

"The wheels of justice don't stop for late hours, Marshal Halverson. How many big cities have night court? How many times did you serve search or seizure warrants at late hours to include holidays and weekends?"

"So I have, counselor. Oh, here's a letter that was delivered to you by the DA's office," said Julie, handing Daniel the envelope.

"Oh, joy, my love letter from Linda," said Daniel as he took the letter and opened it up. He pulled out the contents to see that it was a preliminary copy of the autopsy results on one Geoff Davids. Daniel noted the time of death was estimated to be at 11:30 a.m. and put the envelope into his right, jacket pocket.

"I will go see if your client is awake," said Julie as she went back to the cells. A few minutes later, she returned with Melanie Thompson in her orange jumpsuit and handcuffs.

"Since we do not have an attorney/client room, I'll let you use Marshal Beckman's office," she said, putting Melanie into the office.

"Thank you," said Daniel, closing the door and sitting down in Marshal Beckman's large, red chair.

"Did they read you your rights?" asked Daniel.

"Not yet; how are my boys?" she asked, nervously.

"Fine, but I am charging you for babysitting services."

"I know, I received your bill today when I arrived home. Daniel, I don't know how I'm going to pay you."

"Some mysterious person, who I will catch, seems to be slipping money into my mail slot every time I send you a bill. I highly suspect tomorrow morning I will find a stack of money on the floor in front of my mail slot."

Daniel was silent for a few minutes before he spoke again.

"Where were you at today at 11:30 a.m.?"

"I was still in the car coming off of Red Mountain Pass."

"What time did you get to your house?"

"About 12:15 p.m., I think."

"What happened up to the point you were arrested?"

"That DA woman Linda was talking to me with a large man named Jason Beckman. By the way, he made me very nervous."

"Well, he makes me nervous sometimes, too; continue."

"She asked me a few questions and then I was arrested. I thought I had to have my rights read to me when I was arrested?"

"There is a two pronged test for Miranda. You have to be in custody and being interrogated. Were you free to leave without being blocked by anyone?"

"Well, yes, we were all standing on the porch and I could have gone inside my home or walked down the stairs off the porch."

"And you're sure nobody was blocking you, right?"

"That DA woman was on my left and that big marshal was standing on my right."

"Okay so far, what did Marshal Beckman say to you when he arrested you?"

"You are under arrest; I am charging you with second-degree murder and felony theft of $100,000 from your employer. After that, he put handcuffs on me, put me into the back of this police car and I ended up here."

"Were there any witnesses to this conversation on your porch?"

"No."

"Were you alone in the car you were riding in before you arrived at your home?"

"No, there was special FBI agent Larry Homes and the bank's insurance agent investigating the theft in the car."

"Good, who is Geoff Davids?"

"That was the bank manager. I think someone said he retired a few weeks ago."

"Well, he retired all right. The DA says that you killed him with a blow to the back of the head from a coffee pot. Your fingerprints were found on the coffee pot."

"The only way my fingerprints could have been on that coffee pot was if the coffee pot was one from work or my own home."

"I think the DA is hoping that you will lead them to the money. I don't think the DA has any physical evidence on you, yet. I can get the DA to drop the one charge because you weren't in the area."

"When can I see my boys?"

"Not until after the preliminary hearing. Is there anything else you want to tell me?"

"I have a juvenile record."

"What was the charge?"

"Armed robbery."

"How old were you?"

"Thirteen and running with the wrong crowd. I was in a big city and being rebellious like teenagers and I participated in robbing a convenience store with a really large knife."

"How much did you get?"

"About $30, but it wasn't worth it for what came next over the following years; that was in 1991."

"Where?"

"The State of Tennessee, a small town called Colt. It is about twenty miles or so southwest of the city of Oak Ridge."

"Were those records sealed or expunged or both?"

"I don't know, Daniel."

"Well, rest easy tonight. As your attorney, I will advise you of your Constitutional Rights. If you don't mind, I would like Marshal Halverston to serve as a witness to me reading you your rights."

"Sure, Daniel, that's fine with me."

Daniel stood up and walked over to the office door. He opened it up and waved at Julie. She came over to the door.

"What can I do for you, counselor?" asked Julie.

"I want you to witness me advising my client of her Constitutional Rights."

"Okay, counselor, let me get the form."

Julie disappeared around the corner and opened up a filing cabinet on the far west wall. She returned with a form and entered the office. Julie remained standing while Daniel sat back down again.

"Melanie Thompson, as your duly appointed attorney, I am advising you of your Constitutional rights. Do you understand this?" asked Daniel as he grabbed a pen out of Marshal Beckman's desktop cup.

"Yes, I do."

"Initial the first block, on the left side of the form in front of you," said Daniel as he initialed the right side of the form. He then handed the pen to Melanie. When she was done with it, she handed it back to Daniel.

"You have the right to remain silent. Do you understand this right as I have read it to you?" asked Daniel, initialing in the next block.

"Yes, I do," she replied while initialing.

"If you give up the right to remain silent, anything you say can and will be used against you in a court of law. Do you understand this right as I have read it to you?" asked Daniel, initialing.

"Yes, I do," she said, initialing in the next block.

"You have the right to an attorney and to have that attorney present with you at all stages of questioning. Do you understand this right as I have read it to you?"

"Yes, I do."

"If you cannot afford an attorney, one will be appointed to you at no cost. Do you understand this right as I have read it to you?"

"Yes I do and I know that you are my attorney."

"Having these rights in mind, do you wish to make any statements to law enforcement personnel or the district attorney?"

"No, I do not wish to talk to the police or the district attorney."

"Good answer. Marshal Halverson, I want you to sign the bottom line as a witness and you can put my client back in her cell until her arraignment hearing on Monday," said Daniel as he left the office with a copy of the Miranda rights as Julie put Melanie back into her cell.

The next morning found Daniel back in the courtroom. The jury was still deliberating the fate of his client. Lynn walked into the courtroom and handed Daniel his messages. Sure enough, Lynn had found another stack of sequentially numbered $20 bills in the mail slot along with a $10 bill on the floor. Daniel went downstairs after a few minutes and called Jessica. She took notes and then started planning out her surveillance times. Daniel returned to the courtroom to find Lynn going over some paperwork and Linda smiling at him. Daniel took a sip of his coffee he had bought downstairs and sat at his table with his client.

"Drop the second degree murder charges against my client, Melanie Thompson; she didn't do it," said Daniel, firmly.

"That's what they all say, counselor," replied Linda dryly as she went back to doing some paperwork.

"She has an alibi and it's perfect."

"Don't they all, until the truth comes out either in court or in their statements?"

"She was in an unmarked, GPS equipped, federal police car with an FBI agent and another agent present as witnesses. I can subpoena the GPS records of the car with one phone call."

"Where was she allegedly at when she was in this alleged police car?"

"She was on the top of Red Mountain Pass or just coming off of the south side of it at 11:30 a.m."

"Okay, I'll drop that charge. But, I'm still charging her with the theft of the money from her employer."

"Agreed."

The side door to the courtroom opened and Judge Bishop entered the courtroom. He went directly to his bench and sat down. He then stood up to address the court. The Bailiff went to stand up, but Larry put his left hand up to stop him from doing it. The Bailiff sat back down.

"It appears that the jury has three more questions of the defense. Bailiff, would you please hand the defense these questions?" asked Larry, handing the Bailiff the questions.

The Bailiff handed Daniel the questions. They were simple yes or no questions. Daniel circled the appropriate letters and handed the paper back to the Bailiff. The Bailiff handed the questions back to Larry who quickly left the courtroom and returned later. It was after the lunch break, when the jury was ready for the reading of the verdict. Larry opened the door as the Bailiff stood up.

"All rise, criminal court in the town of Silverton in the State of Colorado for San Juan County is now in session. The Honorable Judge Larry Bishop, presiding."

Larry walked up the stairs to his bench. The jury stood up and handed the Bailiff their verdict. The Bailiff handed the verdict to Judge Bishop. He put on his reading glasses and opened up the piece of paper. He took off his reading glasses and looked over at the jury box.

"Is this the verdict of the jury as a whole?" asked Larry.

"It is, Your Honor," replied the jury foreman, standing up and then sitting back down.

"Very well, will the defendant and his attorney please stand for the reading of the verdict?"

Daniel and his client stood up.

"We, the jury, find the defendant not guilty as charged," said Larry.

"Does the prosecution wish to poll the jury?" asked Larry.

"No, Your Honor, we are satisfied with the jury's verdict."

Daniel turned to face Linda as they both picked up the paperwork.

"When are you going to arraign my client, Melanie Thompson?"

"Monday morning, 9:30 a.m., in Judge Kyle Tillman's courtroom."

"Thank you, Mr. Marcos," said Bill, shaking Daniel's left hand.

"You're welcome, Bill. Now that you're a free man, I think Barry may need you back at work tonight."

Daniel went back to his office with Lynn. Lynn checked over the mail and found her second letter of rejection for law school. She prepared the final bill for Bill Berman and mailed it off that night. When Daniel arrived at home, it looked like a three ring circus going on at his front door. Daniel recognized one of the people as a reporter from the *Ironton Gazette*; Mary Jean. He stepped out of his borrowed car and looked at the front door.

He could see Seth and David trying to get rid of the reporter while dealing with the FBI agent. They were all yelling and screaming at each other when Daniel entered into the fray. He looked at the FBI agent first.

"Mr. Homes, do you have a search warrant or other business on my property?" asked Daniel.

"Not exactly; I was hoping to just politely talk to them. It appears that they don't want to talk to me without your presence."

"Well, I'm here now and my clients definitely don't want to talk to you at this time. Now, if you have no further business with my clients, please leave my property."

After the FBI agent had left, he turned to the face the reporter.

"Let me make this clear to you, exploiting these kids, even for a new story, may be construed in a court of law as a felony offense. The charge could be upped enough to get you labeled as a sex offender."

"That's okay, counselor, I'll leave."

Daniel walked inside his house and shut the door. He locked it and turned to face the kids. They were both scared and nervous at the same time.

"Everyone downstairs in the basement, right now," said Daniel.

Seth spoke first once Daniel had shut the door.

"Is it true what the FBI guy said? That my mom had been arrested when she got back into town?"

"Yes, the DA had your mother arrested."

"Can we see our mother?" asked David.

"Not for a while. She still has to go through the criminal justice process. I have seen her and she is doing fine and sends you her love."

"When can we see her?" asked Todd.

"I told you not for a while. Let me try to explain the criminal justice process to all of you. When your mother was arrested, she was charged with an alleged crime and now must appear before a judge to answer for the alleged crime. This is called an arraignment hearing."

"Okay, so what happens next, Mr. Attorney?" asked David, with some venom in his voice.

"After the arraignment hearing, a date for the preliminary hearing will be set. It is at this hearing, I can ask for a bail bond and your mother should be released on this bail bond to see you. The actual trial date will be set at this hearing as well."

"So, when is she going to this arraignment hearing?" asked Seth.

"On Monday morning. Now, I'm going to try and get visitations arranged for all of you. In the meantime, do not talk to anyone about your mother's case and don't talk to any reporters or law enforcement officials without my presence."

"This other hearing, she could come home afterwards, right?" asked Todd.

"I am going to try my best to have her home for Thanksgiving. But, I don't want any of you to jeopardize it. What the police, the FBI and the DA's office are trying to do is create hate and chaos between you all."

"Why? We didn't do anything wrong and neither did my mom," said David.

"Look, you and I know that, but to them, you're all accomplices and/or accessories to her crime. They hope that by creating discontent, you will lead them to the money and help convict your mother."

"There is no money, Mr. Marcos. But, that is very clever of them to put us against each other," said David.

"Exactly, now let's have dinner, do homework and go to bed after shower."

After dinner and Daniel made sure that their homework was done, he put them all to bed. He sorted out his mail and then sat down on the sofa to map out a plan for Melanie. He looked out the window to see the FBI agent standing on the corner of the street. He let the curtains on the window close before picking up his cell phone. Knowing that his cell phone might be tapped, he called Lynn. He talked to her in a code only they understood.

"Good evening, Lynn, I'll meet you at the office tomorrow. Would you stop by the grocery store and pick up the following items?"

"Sure, what do we need at the office?"

"Some French vanilla-flavored coffee creamer, some fruit and pick up some plastic spoons, please."

"Will do, what time do you want to meet me at the office?"

"About 4:00 p.m.; goodbye."

"Goodbye," she said, hanging up the phone.

Lynn knew the shopping list was bogus. The shopping list was a code for a records check in the state of Tennessee. The rest of the list, plus the time, meant she would actually meet him at the office at 9:00 a.m. with the records check. She logged onto her computer and found what Daniel had asked for; the criminal file on Melanie Thompson.

CHAPTER 11

Daniel fixed the boys breakfast and then took them to his office. He let them go from there so that they could go to their house. There, they brought in the mail and newspapers. They picked up some of their personal items and some more clothes. They returned to Daniel's office and Daniel took them back to his place. He told David to lock the doors and windows, don't let anyone in and don't answer the telephone for any reason.

He returned to the office just as Lynn was opening the door with the grocery bag. The grocery bag had a box of plastic spoons, the coffee creamer container, which was empty, and some oranges and apples made out of wood. They went inside and Lynn handed Daniel the compact disc with Melanie's juvenile file on it. Daniel put the disc into his computer and looked over the file with Lynn right over his shoulder.

"This came from the 22nd judicial district for the State of Tennessee. The results are nolo contendre," said Daniel, closing the file on his computer.

"I think you should drop our client, Daniel," said Lynn.

"No, not yet; Lynn, I want you to call this attorney first thing Monday morning and get him to petition the court to either seal or expunge this record; I don't care which one," said Daniel, passing along the attorney's name.

"Anything else?" She asked, taking the information.

"Please type up a court order to request visitation of my client's children."

"Will do. Daniel; does nolo contendre mean no contest in Latin?"

"Yes, it does, now go type up that court order request while I make a phone call."

As soon as Daniel got off the phone with the duty judge, the phone rang.

"Daniel, this is your answering service Leola here. I have a David Thompson who wants to speak to you."

"Very well, put him through."

There was a pause and a click, then another click. Daniel knew then that the landlines had been tapped. He knew that he would have to be very careful about what he said to David.

"Mr. Marcos, there are a couple people on the property. One is the FBI agent I hit and I don't recognize either of the other two."

"All right, remain calm. Have Seth and your younger brother go to the basement and lock the door. Tell them don't come out until either I get there, the Silverton Town Marshal gets there or the San Juan County Sheriff's Department gets there."

"Okay, I'll tell them," said David as he put his left hand over the speaker. "It's done, now what?"

"Ask the FBI agent through the door if he has either a search or seizure warrant."

"Okay," said David.

Silence for a few seconds.

"He says he has a search warrant."

"Okay, tell him to put that search or seizure warrant up against the window next to the door; read it carefully and double-check the address and date of issue."

Silence again as Lynn walked into the room. Daniel pointed at her and wrote something down on a notepad. He handed it to her and motioned her out of the room. Lynn immediately called the Silverton Town Marshal's office.

"It looks good to me."

"Now, I want you to check the FBI agent's badge. Have him hold it up to the same window."

Silence once again. Lynn opened the door and put her left thumb up in the air.

"Okay, looks good to me," said David, who was starting to get nervous.

"Ask the other two persons to see their badges. Check their badges to see if any one of them is a U.S. Marshal."

"Okay." Again there was silence.

"No, they all say FBI."

"Then, politely, but firmly, tell them that without a U.S. Marshal present, they cannot serve the warrants. If they do barge in, then any evidence taken will probably be ruled inadmissible in court. But, don't tell them that last line."

"Okay," again silence for a few seconds; then the phone was hung up.

"Lynn, bring me a hammer," said Daniel as he put the CD of his client's criminal file into an envelope which he smashed into pieces. He tossed the CD pieces into the trashcan. The phone was ringing once again; he didn't recognize the number.

"Hello?" asked Daniel.

"Mr. Marcos, this is duty U.S. Atty. Dick Waddell. I should have you arrested for obstructing justice and interfering in police business."

"Well, Mr. Waddell, if you want to arrest me and the kids for such things, go ahead. Before you issue the warrants, let me tell you something."

"If it is about the agents and the warrants, I know. I was able to get those warrants signed last night."

"But you failed to make sure that a U.S. Marshal was present to serve those warrants. I could prove in federal court that you failed to follow proper policy and procedure, committed negligence and did not exercise due diligence."

"You might be able to prove those things."

"Which, when I prove them in court, the evidence obtained during the search is inadmissible in court. As I see it, you have only two choices."

"Which are?"

"Call off those FBI agents or find a U.S. Marshal. The closest U.S. Marshal to Silverton is in Grand Junction. The next closest is Farmington, New Mexico. Either way, you're looking at several hours before anyone can get here."

"You hold on the line. I think your statements are ludicrous, but I'll call the duty judge. I will then call you back."

"I'll be waiting," said Daniel, hanging up the phone.

About half an hour later, the US Atty. called Daniel back.

"Hello, Mr. Waddell, I've been waiting for your phone call," said Daniel.

"Mr. Marcos, it appears that the duty judge, Her Honor Krysta Johnson, agrees with you. There is a U.S. Marshal enroute from Farmington, New Mexico. She'll be there by 7:00 p.m.; is that going to make you happy?"

"Very happy, I'm looking forward to seeing her," said Daniel, hanging up the phone.

Daniel went back to his place to find it quiet. He unlocked the door and went inside. He didn't hear anyone moving around, so he went downstairs to the basement. Using his keys, he opened the door. After letting them all out of the basement, he fixed them all lunch. After lunch, it was time to do laundry. Once laundry was completed, he gathered them all around the table.

"David, I'm proud of you. You did really well today. Now, I have some important business to conduct in Durango. I should be back by 7:00 p.m., if I am not, David, make sure to check to see if those FBI agents brought along a U.S. Marshal."

"I will and I'll remember to put my brothers down in the basement."

"Good, now I'm off to Durango."

A little before 7:00 p.m., Daniel returned to find FBI agents, a U.S. Marshal and the news were all there. Daniel pushed through the crowd and into his home. He closed the door and gathered the kids together.

"David, do you have your driver's license?"

"Yes, I do."

"Here are the keys to the car in the driveway. Take your brothers here to the Ironton Town Marshal's office. Marshal Beckman is expecting you," said Daniel handing David the car keys and a copy of the court order.

"Anything else you want to tell me, Mr. Marcos?" asked David, taking the keys and a copy of the court order.

"Make sure everyone is buckled up and drive under the speed limit; they will be following you. Expect to get checked for weapons, drugs and evidence, when you leave the house."

"Okay, Seth let's go," said David as everyone left the house.

The FBI agents burst in the door and shoved the search and seizure warrants into Daniel's face. Daniel smiled, took the paperwork and started reading through it. The U.S. Marshal entered into the house a few seconds later, showed Daniel her badge and then simply glared at him. Daniel could tell she was very angry.

"Are you happy, Mr. Marcos, attorney at law? Because of you, I had to leave Elephant Butte Reservoir with a stringer full of largemouth bass attached to the boat!" she said angrily as she answered her cell phone.

Daniel saw the FBI agents taking his computer and other pieces of evidence. As they were leaving, the marshal found out she was stranded in Silverton for the night. She hung up her cell phone and turned to face Daniel.

"Mr. Marcos, you are really on my garbage list now. It looks like I'm stuck here," she said.

"I'm terribly sorry about that Marshal Lucas; are you hungry?"

"Yes, I am. Are you trying to take me out on a date, Mr. Marcos? I'm warning you, I am armed and I won't hesitate to shoot you."

"I completely understand that one. If I may suggest, there is a lovely café that is still open, next to the Silverton Town Marshal's office. I will buy you dinner, put you up in the bed-and-breakfast across the street and make sure that you get out of here on the first train back to Durango at 7:15 a.m. I will do all of this at my expense."

"I accept, let's go."

Monday morning arrived too soon for Daniel. He fixed the boys breakfast and made sure they got to school. He then went to his office and found Lynn counting another stack of money. She walked past Daniel and drove to the bank to make the deposit. Daniel poured himself a cup of coffee and started going through his messages. Most of the messages were routine. He sat down at his desk, when the phone rang.

"Hello, Attorney Daniel Marcos speaking, how can I help you?"

"This is Linda, Daniel. Your client's case number is 15CR29; have a nice day," said Linda, hanging up the phone. Daniel hung up his receiver as Lynn entered the office.

"Lynn, we now have a case number to put on Melanie Thompson's file. The case number is 15CR29; file the Discovery Motions paperwork and make sure we follow all the provisions of Rule 41."

"Will do," she said as she left to go to her desk. A few minutes later, Jessica entered the office.

"Jessica, have you found out who's been paying my client's legal fees?" asked Daniel, taking out a pen from the pen holder on his desk and grabbing a legal pad next to the telephone.

"Yes, the vehicle's license plate is registered to a Bill Edgeworth; is he a client of yours?"

"Not that I recall, but I will have Lynn check my records."

"I've been in contact with the insurance agent investigating the alleged theft from the bank. He's still convinced your client did it, but he can't figure out how."

"Well, let him keep chasing his tail around in circles. Now be on your way, but keep your eye on him; I still smell an insurance scam."

"Okay."

She left as Lynn returned. She started filling out all the paperwork that Daniel had asked her to do. When she completed it, she took it into Daniel for a review. Daniel made the necessary changes and then handed the paperwork back to her. She went to the bank to get the paperwork notarized. She then filled out the wire form for the attorney in Tennessee. She returned to the office, handed Daniel the paperwork and the wire receipt.

"Lynn, check our files and see if we've ever had a client by the name of Bill Edgeworth."

"Right away."

She left his office and started searching through the files. Daniel looked up at the clock on the wall; 9:30 a.m. Daniel's client would be in Judge Kyle Tillman's courtroom, right now, being arraigned. Judge Kyle Tillman was looking over the case file and trying to make sense of it. He looked down at Melanie Thompson from his bench.

"Will the defendant, Melanie Thompson in the case number 15CR29, please rise?"

Melanie, dressed in an orange jumpsuit and clad in handcuffs and leg irons, stood up.

"Since this is the arraignment part of your judicial process, this hearing will be informal. All I ask of you, Mrs. Thompson is that you address me as Your Honor. Do you understand this?"

"Yes, Your Honor, I do."

"Very well, are you aware of the charge against you?"

"Yes, Your Honor."

"What is this charge?"

"The district attorney and the Ironton Town Marshal advised me that I was being charged with violating Colorado revised statutes 18-4-401, Section 2, Paragraph D for the theft of $100,000 from my employer."

"Are you aware, or have you been told, of the penalty if you are convicted of this crime?"

"Yes, Your Honor. I was told by the district attorney that the penalty could be life in prison without parole at the Eastern Correctional Facility for women outside of Canyon City, Colorado, or I could get twelve years for the Class III felony."

"Do you have legal representation?"

"Yes, Your Honor."

"Have you been advised of your Constitutional rights?"

"I have been advised of my constitutional rights by my attorney."

"Do you want me to read you your rights again?"

"No, Your Honor, I have had my rights read to me and I understand them."

"So noted. Mrs. Thompson, you are being charged with one count of violating Colorado revised statutes 18-4-401, Section 2, Paragraph D, theft in the amount of $100,000; how do you plead?"

"Not guilty, Your Honor."

"So noted. Let the court records show that the defendant pleaded not guilty to the charge. A preliminary hearing will be set for next week on November 12th at 1:15 p.m. The defendant is hereby remanded back to the custody of the Ironton Town Marshal," said Judge Kyle Tillman, banging down his gavel.

Lynn entered Daniel's office to talk to him. She had the mail in her hand which contained the third letter of rejection from the various law schools she had applied to over the past few months.

Daniel knew, from the look on her face, she had received yet another rejection letter.

"Let me guess, Lynn, another rejection letter?" asked Daniel, nicely.

"Yes and we have never had a client by the name of Bill Edgeworth."

"Okay and keep filling out those applications, you will be successful. It took me over twenty times before I was accepted."

"Thank you, Daniel."

"Now, I'm going to go check on our client," said Daniel as he left the office. He walked down the street and across the next block to the Ironton Town Marshal's office.

"Good afternoon, Mr. Marcos, what can I do for you?" asked Jason as he stood up from behind the counter.

"I'd like to see my client."

"I'll let you use my office."

A few minutes later, in handcuffs, Marshal Beckman put Melanie into his office; she remained standing. Marshal Beckman shut the door.

"Hello, Melanie, how are you feeling?" asked Daniel.

"Okay, I guess. I've been feeling a little sick recently, but I think I can handle it."

"Did they give you a date for your preliminary hearing?"

"Yes, next Monday, November 12th."

"Have you told Marshal Beckman that you have been feeling ill?"

"No, because I think it's all the stress I'm under from being in a place like this and being away from my kids."

"Well, you may be right. Do you have a primary care physician?"

"Yes, Dr. Penny Roberts."

"I'll have your primary care physician come check on you."

"Okay."

"Who is Bill Edgeworth?"

"The bank president; why?"

"I found out who's been paying your legal fees. I have a suspicion that either he or one of his representatives will be at your preliminary hearing to assist you with posting bail."

"Why is he paying my legal fees?"

"I don't know; maybe he likes you. I'll talk to you later."

Daniel left the marshal's office and returned to his office. He then went home to see the boys. After dinner, Daniel called Dr. Penny Roberts' office since she was the only general practitioner in Ironton. He left a message with her answering service to check on his client in the Ironton jail. Daniel hung up the phone and went to bed.

CHAPTER 12

The day of the preliminary hearing had arrived. Daniel found themselves in court with his client, the FBI agent and the insurance company fraud investigator, Kyle Coats. Daniel also saw that Melanie's kids were in the courtroom. There were a few others in the courtroom that Daniel didn't recognize.

Just before court started, Jessica Kim entered the courtroom, handed Daniel a note and then left rather abruptly. Daniel reviewed the note and then folded it back up. He then placed the note into his left jacket pocket. The Bailiff stood up along with the rest of the courtroom.

"All rise, criminal court for the town of Silverton in San Juan County for the State of Colorado's 6th judicial district is now in session. The Honorable Judge Kyle Tillman presiding over case number 15CR29," said Sergio.

Judge Kyle Tillman walked up a few steps to his bench, opened up the case file and sat down at his bench.

"You may be seated," he said as the courtroom sat down. He looked over at Daniel and then at Linda.

"This is the preliminary hearing in the case number 15CR29. Let the court records show that the prosecution is present. The defense counsel is also present along with the defendant. I will ask defense counsel if he objects to the prosecution starting off these proceedings, which includes a request for reasonable bail?"

"No objections, Your Honor, "said Daniel, standing up and then sitting back down.

"Very well, what evidence does the prosecution have to present to this court in connection with this case?"

"We are ready, Your Honor, with prosecution exhibits A, B, C and D."

"Very well."

"Objection, Your Honor. I have seen the prosecution's evidence and I demand a suppression of the prosecution's exhibits A, B, C and D," said Daniel, standing up and then sitting back down.

"Prosecution?"

"We object to defense counsel's demand!"

"Will defense counsel explain to this court why they wish to have an evidence suppression hearing on the prosecution's exhibits?"

"Not in open court, Your Honor."

"Very well, this court will recess while I talk to both counselors in my chambers."

Everyone stood up as the judge, Linda and Daniel left the courtroom. Once they were inside of the judge's chambers, they remained standing while Judge Kyle Tillman sat down at his small desk. He took out a small legal pad and a pen out of the upper left desk drawer. Judge Kyle Tillman looked straight at Daniel.

"Okay, Mr. Marcos, Esquire, why are the prosecution's exhibits so bad to you and your client?" asked Judge Kyle Tillman.

"Prosecution Exhibit A is the vault logbook. My client's position as the bank teller supervisor makes her responsible for signing that logbook each and every time she gets into the vault. Therefore, that evidence is both inculpatory and exculpatory to my client."

"Prosecution, that logbook could be viewed by an appellate court as such."

"I demand the evidence stay, Your Honor. If you want to steal something, might as well put the evidence of the theft out in the open," said Linda.

"All right, I'll let it stay until the trial," said Daniel.

"What about Exhibit B?" asked Judge Kyle Tillman.

"Your Honor, a couple of money bags, from the Federal Reserve Bank, with my client's bank name and routing ID number on them, doesn't prove anything. So what if my client's fingerprints are on them."

"I'll move for suppression on that one if the prosecution does not object," said Judge Kyle Tillman.

"We have no objections, Your Honor."

"What about Exhibit C? This is your client's criminal file."

"Which, Your Honor, is or was sealed and can only be opened by Your Honor. However, my esteemed colleague here, in obtaining this evidence, has violated my client's Fourth Amendment right; protection from an illegal search and seizure."

"Prosecution?"

"I obtained the criminal file from a reliable source, Your Honor," said Linda.

"She illegally obtained it, Your Honor, from an FBI raid on my home. The information was on my hard drive, but the search warrant that the FBI served me made no mention of the internal parts of the computer."

"Hogwash, Your Honor, defense counsel is trying to confuse you."

"Can you prove to me that this information was illegally obtained?"

"I certainly can, Your Honor. Here's a copy of the search warrant," said Daniel, handing over his copy of the warrant. Judge Kyle Tillman looked it over and then handed it back to Daniel, who put it into his right jacket pocket.

"Go on, Mr. Marcos."

"The search warrant makes no mention of looking at the contents of a hard drive. Since the hard drive is inside of the computer casing – therefore, another barrier – another search warrant would be needed; it is a judicial fact."

"Your Honor, he's trying to confuse you, again. Don't buy any of this judicial fact crap," said Linda.

"Can the defense counsel cite any legal decisions where such was the case?" asked Judge Kyle Tillman.

"I certainly can, Your Honor. Case number 98CR18186, 2nd Federal Circuit Court, Judge Ryan Kelly presiding over a child pornography case. The judge agreed with the defense counsel on the computer issue and suppressed the evidence gained by it."

"Prosecution, that search warrant made no mention of the contents of the hard drive. Until I can confirm what defense counsel has told me, the evidence is suppressed; now what about Exhibit D?"

"It is a known fact that there are hundreds of ways to defeat or confuse that particular polygraph test that my client was given. In fact, that polygraph test today is now less than ten percent accurate. The same set of questions was used by my private investigator to give the CVSA polygraph test. I want my test results submitted."

"Prosecution, I'm inclined to agree with defense counsel. It would seem to show to an appellate court judge that you willfully violated the defendant's Sixth Amendment right to see the evidence being held against them."

"Very well, Your Honor. I will allow the evidence to be presented," said Linda.

"Okay, now let's all head back to the courtroom to discuss bail," said Tillman.

Everyone returned to the courtroom. Judge Kyle Tillman made some phone calls and looked up a few other cases before returning to the courtroom. Judge Tillman walked into the courtroom and looked down at both Daniel and Linda.

"Defense, I'm letting Exhibits A, B and D stay part of the case, contingent upon the stipulations from me in writing as to what I will accept or not accept in my courtroom; is that clear, prosecution?"

"Yes, Your Honor, it is very clear," said Linda.

"As for exhibit C, the evidence was illegally obtained and therefore does not exist in the eyes of the court. This conclusion stems from the court case in 1998 that defense counsel cited in my chambers, a review of similar cases in this Federal Circuit Court that Colorado belongs to and a phone call to Federal Circuit Court Judge Krysta Johnson backed up by defense counsel's demand. Now, is the prosecution ready to move on to a bail discussion?"

"The prosecution is ready," said Linda as she remained standing.

"Proceed."

"The prosecution requests that, due to the nature of the crime, bail be denied to the defendant. She has hidden, somewhere, a large enough sum of money to escape this court's jurisdiction; never to return. She also has a passport for herself and her kids."

"Defense?"

"My client requests reasonable bail be set. She has none of the money she allegedly stole and if she did have this money, she could have fled a long time ago with her kids."

"Objection, Your Honor. She has paid over $20,000 in legal fees to defense counsel," said Linda.

"Your Honor, my client's legal fees have been paid by an anonymous donor and all this, Your Honor, was done while she was in jail."

"I see. Given the nature of the crime, the own recognizance bond is out of the question. However, bail will be set at $650,000; dismissed until April 26th for the trial."

"Thank you, Your Honor," said Linda.

Bill Edgeworth waited until almost everyone was gone before he approached Daniel; Daniel was closing up his briefcase, getting ready to leave, himself.

"Mr. Marcos, do you have time to answer some questions?" asked Bill.

"Sure."

"How much is the bail bond?"

"Thirty percent or $216,667.00."

"Who do I pay it to?"

"The clerk of the court downstairs."

"Thank you for keeping my donations a secret."

"Not a problem."

"Can she return to work?"

"As soon as you post her bail. Can I make sure that she calls me a couple times a day just to be safe?"

"I will ensure it, Mr. Marcos and I will pay another legal fee for her if it becomes necessary. If you need anything from me, just call or visit the bank."

"I will, Mr. Edgeworth."

Daniel returned to his office. Lynn had already called Jessica so she was waiting at the office. They all walked into Daniel's inner office and Jessica shut the door. Lynn took out a pen and prepared to take notes while Jessica prepared for her assignment as well. Daniel stared at the ceiling for a while before speaking.

"Our client is not guilty of the crime. I was able to get her previous criminal file ruled inadmissible. Jessica, here is what

I want you to do," said Daniel, looking at the wall instead of the ceiling.

"Go ahead, Daniel, I'm ready," she said.

"I want you to gather up all the information you can on the bank. Gather up information on the current employees, etc. Jessica, I smell an insurance scam, so be looking for the clues," said Daniel.

"Will do."

"Be on your way."

As soon as Jessica left, Daniel looked straight at Lynn.

"Lynn, call my client to come see me for her official statement. Make sure to call Linda about what questions she wants to ask my client. If Linda wants, she can be present to ask the questions."

"Okay."

"I also want you to have Mr. Coats come in here to see me. Set up an appointment with Mr. Edgeworth next week at, say, 9:30 a.m."

"Will do; anything else?"

"Yes, there is, call Jessica on her cell phone and tell her to keep a close eye on Mr. Coats."

"Will do."

Daniel looked out the window. There were dark gray clouds coming in over the mountains.

"Lynn, get all that stuff done right now. Then go home, I'll take care of locking up shop and I'll see you on Monday."

The first of many snowstorms had arrived at the towns of Ironton and Silverton. The storm brought sixteen inches of snow to Ironton and twelve inches of snow to Silverton. Bitter cold followed this snowstorm and when Monday came around, the wind had started to blow, making it even colder. When Daniel arrived at work, the sun was shining and the temperature was minus four without wind chill. Daniel entered the office to find Lynn taking care of paperwork.

"Good morning, Lynn. Have you heard from Jessica, yet?" asked Daniel, taking off his heavy jacket, hat, boots and gloves.

"Not yet, but our client called to let us know she was already at work," she replied, holding a piece of paper in her left hand. Daniel looked at it and knew it was another reject letter.

"Another reject letter, Lynn?"

"Yes, Daniel and it's the tenth one so far."

"It can be a little frustrating; all I can say is patience will pay off."

"Thank you, Daniel. I will keep applying."

"Have you applied to the Denver University's law school? They've expanded the program considerably since I went there. They used to only offer law degrees in environmental, business and corporate law."

"What do they offer now?"

"Well, I was the first lawyer to go through their criminal Law program. The last time I received one of their flyers, they now offer law degrees in personal injury law, Constitutional law, real estate law, copyrights, trademarks and patents law and I think divorce law now. Browse through one of the flyers next time they come in the mail."

"Okay, I will do that, Daniel."

Daniel went into his inner office and started his daily routine. Jessica showed up at 8:15 a.m. with a whole bunch of information for Daniel. Lynn showed Jessica into Daniel's inner office and shut the door. She set all the paperwork down on the floor. She reached in the top box of paperwork and pulled out her reference notes.

"Daniel, where do you want to start?" asked Jessica as she organized her notes.

"The bank employees."

"The first one, teller Amy Peters, has been there for over ten years. She's also one of the only living relatives of Mr. Roger Peters of Peters Ammunition Company. We know that company as Remington Ammunition and Firearms, Inc., today," she said, handing Daniel the reference note. Daniel took it and looked it over before setting it down on his desk.

"I gather she has a trust fund of some kind?"

"Yes, held by a very prestigious law firm in South Bridgeport, Connecticut. Current value, $29.6 million."

"Looks like we can eliminate her from the list of suspects; who's next?"

"Carl Jeffers is next in line to take over the position of bank manager. He holds multiple degrees of bachelor's level or higher

117

in finance, business, business administration and accounting. Also has a big crush on our client," she said, handing Daniel the reference note.

"Okay, sounds like we can eliminate him from the list; next?"

"The dead bank manager, Geoff Davids. He held three masters degrees, in accounting, finance and business operations. Worked his entire life in the banking industry," she said, handing over her reference note.

"Where else did he work at, besides the Ironton Town Bank and Trust?"

"The mint in San Francisco, California and the mint in Philadelphia, Pennsylvania. He also worked at the Treasury Department, the Federal Reserve Banks of Cleveland, New York, Dallas, Minneapolis, Kansas City and the branch office here in Denver," she said, handing over the reference note.

"Who's last?"

"The bank president, Bill Edgeworth. Now, here's where it gets really interesting."

"How interesting does it get?"

"Mr. Edgeworth Merritt, the last surviving child of Mr. and Mrs. Jack Busey."

"If my memory serves me right, the Busey family founded the town of Ironton on April 2nd of 1887."

"That is correct, Daniel. The town's original bank was in a general store where the parking lot for City Hall is located."

"Tell me about the bank building."

"The Ironton Town Bank and Trust building we see today is not the original. That is the fourth building. However, the building has a colorful history," she said, handing Daniel a large, thick file folder. Daniel set it down on the side of his desk for a later thorough review.

"Tell me about this colorful history," said Daniel.

"It is all in my thorough report, but I'll hit the highlights," said Jessica pulling out her summary sheet off the top of the next pile of papers in the box she had brought in earlier.

"Construction began on the first Ironton Town Bank building on May 4th, 1887 and it was completed on April 30th, 1888. The doors opened on May 1, 1888. The bank was robbed on May 14, 1888.

The paper money, gold bars, etc. and five strong boxes, were never recovered. It appears that the bandits simply disappeared with their loot."

"When was the next colorful part of this bank's history?"

"The very next morning, May 15, 1888, the building burned to the ground. The fire was blamed on the senior teller who accidently knocked over an oil lamp of some kind."

"I surmise the building was insured and rebuilt?"

"Yes, the building was insured, as was the contents of the vault, by an insurance company out of Denver called Lane and Beggars."

"What happened to that insurance company?"

"They went out of business on June 17, 1913. This was the day after the bank burned to the ground after the second robbery on June 15, 1913. The money, gold bars, etc. and three strong boxes this time was never recovered."

"Keep going, Jessica. Who was the new insurance company that took over?"

"A company called Occidental Casualty Insurance Company. They were allegedly based out of Salt Lake City, Utah."

"What do you mean allegedly based out of Salt Lake City, Utah?"

"I really couldn't seem to find anything in the state of Utah's records in reference to the company."

"Well, it's not surprising, considering back then they didn't really keep really great records; go on."

"The bank was robbed again on August 8, 1934. That was a Friday. On Monday morning, the whole building had fallen into an old mine shaft of the Chadd Mine Company. The vault fell into a large, deep hole and had to be declared a total loss because of the debris in the way."

"I surmise that the insurance company went out of business the day after the disaster; right?"

"Yes, the bank building was moved to its present location that we see today and renamed the Ironton Town Bank and Trust, on September 2, 1934."

"I surmise the property was fully insured once again by a new insurance company?"

"Yes, the FDIC of course ensures the bank deposits up to $250,000. Banks can buy more insurance for a higher premium, up to $15 million in aggregate total. The insurance company that insures the property today is none other than Bowker and Bowker, LLC out of New York City."

"How much is the property insured for at this time?"

"The official report is $10,500,000."

"Jessica, be on standby for some more investigating. When was the last robbery?"

"Until your client allegedly robbed it, September 9, 1951. The money was never recovered."

"Be on your way; Lynn, forward the phones to the answering service and bring along your notepad."

Jessica left with Daniel and Lynn. Daniel and Lynn arrived at the Ironton Town Bank and Trust building a little before 9:30 a.m. They ran into Mr. Kyle Coats as he was leaving the bank. Daniel smiled and looked right at him. Mr. Coats purposefully ignored Daniel and Lynn, looking right past them.

"Mr. Coats, I need to talk to you in my office; can I set up an appointment time for you?" asked Daniel.

"I'm not talking to you, counselor; have a nice day," he said as he continued down the steps and stepped into his car.

"Not very chatty is he?" asked Lynn.

"He was avoiding me, Lynn. That tells me that he's got something to hide."

They entered the bank to talk to Mr. Edgeworth.

CHAPTER 13

Bill Edgeworth took both Daniel and Lynn into his private office. After he had shut the door, he used his right hand to point to the chairs in front of his desk. He sat down behind his desk and smiled at the both of them. Lynn, pulling out her notepad and a pen, prepared to take down the answers to Daniel's questions.

"Good morning, Counselor. Need a cup of coffee to warm up?" asked Bill.

"That would be nice," said Daniel turning to his left to find a complete coffee cart. Daniel and Lynn helped themselves and then sat back down.

"What can I do for you?" asked Bill, smiling.

"If it is all right with you, I'll ask you some questions and Lynn will write down the answers. Please forgive me if I ask some off the wall questions," said Daniel, gathering his thoughts.

"That's all right by me and I don't think Melanie committed the theft."

"I don't think she did either, but proving it could be a challenge."

"I hear you on that one. What questions can I possibly answer for you?" asked Bill.

"You were married to Jacklyn Busey, weren't you?" asked Daniel.

"Yes, we were married on February 14th, 1963. She passed away of an unusual and rare form of aggressive cancer on February 15th, 2008."

"Forty-five years of marriage, that's quite an accomplishment, Mr. Edgeworth."

"Why, thank you, Counselor. We had seven children and now we have four grandchildren; she was a good, strong woman to me."

"You're welcome; what do you know of the robberies that occurred at this bank?"

"Mostly rumors and some incomplete stories that both my father and grandfather told me as a kid."

"How about the first robbery that occurred on May 14th, 1888?"

"Not much to tell except for the fact that the bank burnt to the ground the next morning. The bandits simply disappeared into the woods and the loot was never recovered."

"How much did those bandits get away with at that time?"

"Several strong boxes containing paper money, other negotiables and gold bullion in the form of 24kt ingots. In fact, those strong boxes had to weigh hundreds of pounds each with the gold in there."

"When the building burnt to the ground, was the vault damaged?"

"No, the vaults then, unlike today, were both air and water tight as well as fireproof, drill proof and pretty resilient to even the explosives used at that time."

"Money-wise, what did the bandits get away with?"

"About $20,000.00 in cash with some bonds, sureties and other negotiables, which, if found in good condition, would be priceless to numismatics collectors. The Government Services Administration still owns them to this day. If you find them, I might be able to get the Treasury Department to pay you back interest payments," said Bill, laughing, which made Daniel and Lynn laugh as well.

"What about the gold bullion?"

"About $15,000.00 by that day's standards."

"So, the insurance company paid off on a $35,000.00 loss plus rebuilding costs; that's a nice chunk of change even back then. How much would that gold be worth today if it is recovered in good condition?"

"Well, if it is still in the strong boxes and in good condition, more than $10,000,000.00. In fact, I can tell you the exact price to within a few dollars," said Bill, picking up the phone on his desk. He called his new bank manager, Carl Jeffers and talked to him for a few minutes. Bill then punched the numbers into a calculator he had sitting on the left side of his desk.

"By today's prices, with gold currently selling on the market at $1,195.00 an ounce, that gold would be worth $13,765,949.00."

"And the fire was blamed on the head teller, right?"

"Yes, I believe that the person said they had accidently knocked over an oil or kerosene lamp of the time."

"The second robbery on June 15th, 1913; how much was taken and what happened?"

"Basic bank robbery of the time, bandits fled with six strong boxes once again. Those boxes were filled with coins, currency of the time, stocks, bonds and other negotiables and more gold bullion. The value then was about $75,000.00."

"Let me guess, the place burnt to the ground again the next day; right? The insurance company paid off on the loss and the rebuilding; right? Oh, let me guess, the head teller was blamed for this accident as well?"

"Yes, to all of those questions, but the arson investigator checked the electrical wiring. He found it had been damaged, probably during installation and that's what caused the fire. The money would be worth a fortune to those collectors looking for such fine examples for their collections."

"Do you know who the executor of the old Busey Estate is?"

"Me, Counselor; when Dale Busey passed away, everything was handed over to my late wife. Of course, when she passed away, everything became mine."

"How much did the vault weigh?"

"From the paperwork I found in the attic of this old building, about thirty tons. It took twelve horses and four mules to put it into place when it arrived in Ironton."

"Do you have the combination to the vault?"

"No, I don't have the combination to that vault. You are aware that that vault fell into a mineshaft?"

"Yes, sometime in 1934, I believe. Fell in after a robbery over a holiday weekend. I believe the date was August 8th, 1934."

"Yes, the bank was closed because everyone in town was celebrating Colorado Week. We didn't find out what had happened until the following Tuesday, August 11th, 1934."

"At that time, as the owner of the bank, you would have had a key to the front doors, teller drawers, the vault, etc.?"

"Yes, but the vault requires a key and combination to get into it."

"So, this building has been here since 1934, then?"

"Yes, the old vault had to be replaced, of course. The repair job was really expensive, for that time. Remember, that was during the Great Depression and Prohibition had just ended. The repair cost was almost $100,000.00."

"Ah, yes, the 21st Amendment had just been ratified. What happened after the September 9th, 1951 robbery and how much did the bandits get away with at the time?"

"The bandits ran off into the hills behind the bank here and disappeared with over $4,000,000.00 in cash."

"That seems like a lot of money, what did they do, clean out the vault?"

"No, as a young bank teller myself, my teller drawer had about $250,000.00 in cash in it up until January 1st, 1969. The bandits took my teller drawer and five other teller drawers at the same time, at gunpoint."

"What's so special about January 1st, 1969?"

"On that day, the Treasury Department, under orders from then President Lyndon B. Johnson, was ordered to pull from circulation and destroy all cash notes above $100.00. My teller drawer had spots for the $500.00, $1,000.00, $5,000.00 and $10,000.00 cash notes."

"I see and the bank is insured by the Federal Deposit Insurance Corporation?"

"Yes, through Bowker and Bowker, LLC. As a small town bank, the FDIC doesn't insure you except through a third party. All accounts in this bank are guaranteed up to a minimum of $250,000.00 per insured customer. I also make sure that the insurance premiums are paid every month so that in aggregate total, this bank's depositors are insured up to my current maximum of $6,500,000.00."

"What happened after the 1951 bank robbery?"

"My office fell into an old mine tunnel from the Chadd mine, I believe. The tunnel had to be filled in five times to fill it up completely. In 1983, my office and the outer door to the entrance to the bank fell into that same hole again."

"Did they ever fix that problem?"

"Oh, yes, the repair cost was over $3,000,000.00 because the construction company had to drive steel pylons over three hundred seventy-five feet into the ground to reach bedrock. The building sits on shocks and a sub-floor before the main floor which we are all standing on right now."

"Who made the original vault?"

"According to the design plans of this building, a company called the Schenectady New York Bronze and Ironworks."

"Did the vault have a serial number?"

"Yes, the serial number was two fifteen. By the way, treasure hunters for over 100 years have been coming up here looking for that loot; none of them has ever been successful."

"Okay, if I need anything further, I'll call you. By the way, can I see the old bank manager's office?"

"Sure, it is the office that is next to the back entrance to the teller line. Mr. Marcos, I never really liked Mr. Davids very much."

"Why is that, Mr. Edgeworth?"

"He seemed a little crooked to me."

"I'll keep that in mind, thank you."

Daniel and Lynn left his office. Daniel opened up the office door, turned on the lights and looked around. He could see where the coffee maker had been at by the indentations left behind in the carpet. Daniel closed the door after turning off the lights. He and Lynn went back to the office and then to lunch. After lunch, Lynn began typing up the questions and answers. When she had finished them, she took them into Daniel for his review.

"Good job, Lynn. Make two copies; take one to Mr. Edgeworth and have him sign that one which he can keep. Have him sign the other one and we will keep that one as a possible defense exhibit."

"Yes, Daniel; is there anything else?"

"Call my client and call Jessica; I want to see both of them."

"Yes, Daniel."

Jessica showed up first. Lynn informed Daniel that Mr. Coats was very busy and could not talk to Daniel. Melanie called Lynn and told her she would be there after she got off work. As Jessica was walking into Daniel's office, Linda called; Lynn put her through.

"What can I do for you Linda?" asked Daniel as he grabbed a small legal pad and setting down the box that Jessica had brought in earlier.

"I plan on being in your office tomorrow morning to interrogate your client; thank you and goodbye," said Linda, hanging up the phone as Daniel put the pad away. He motioned for Jessica to come inside; she shut the door.

"Take some notes," said Daniel.

Jessica pulled out a small pad of paper from her briefcase and a pen from her left inside jacket pocket.

"Go ahead, Daniel," she said.

"I want copies of the *Ironton Gazette* for the days following each of the bank robberies as well as any information on the repairs to the bank in the 1980s."

"Anything else?"

"See if this company is still in business and if it is, I want the combination to that vault's serial number," he said handing her the notes he had taken earlier that day.

"Anything else?" she asked, taking the note.

"Find the maps of the actual or proposed mine shafts and tunnels of the old Chadd mine. Also, see if you can get pictures of the properties surrounding the old Busey Estate. When you get those, bring them into me."

"Will do; do you have anything else for me to do?"

"No, that's all; be on your way."

Melanie entered the outer office and walked into Daniel's inner office. Daniel looked up and had her sit down in a chair in front of his desk. Lynn shut the door.

"Melanie, the DA called me a few minutes ago. She said she wants to interrogate you at 8:00 a.m. tomorrow morning; be here at 7:45 a.m."

"Okay, I'll be here."

"By the way, what are in those boxes you keep sending me?" asked Daniel.

"The serial numbers of all the $50 and $100 bills that came through my drawer. I had a computer program that allowed me to wirelessly scan those bills."

"That may be to your advantage; dismissed."

Melanie left Daniel's office. Daniel sat back in his comfortable office chair and devised a plan to get Melanie off the hook. He also thought how he could make Melanie a new woman. He had noticed she put on some weight but thought better of saying anything about it to her. Daniel stepped out into his outer office.

"Lynn, get in touch with Mr. Coats. Tell him I need to talk to him and tell him I'll make it worth his while," said Daniel.

"Okay," she said, picking up the phone.

A few minutes before 5:00 p.m., Mr. Coats showed up at Daniel's office. Lynn was leaving and so Mr. Coats and Daniel entered Daniel's inner office. Daniel used his left hand to point to one of the three chairs in Daniel's office; Mr. Coats sat down in the chair to the left of Daniel's desk. Daniel sat down in his chair and looked right at Mr. Coats.

"Your secretary said you would make it worth my while; so here I am," said Mr. Coats.

"How would you like to be a multimillionaire?" asked Daniel.

Mr. Coats raised his eyebrows a little.

"What do I have to do to become one?"

"Two things; first drop the charges against my client. Second, split the money with her, Mr. Edgeworth and yourself."

"How do I know that you will keep your end of the bargain?"

"I will provide you, anonymously of course, with the location to the bank vault. The bank vault contains about $30 million in gold bullion alone."

"The money from those robberies has never been recovered."

"That's because the money and other negotiables in those strong boxes never left the vault. By the way, the government services administration still has a reward out on it; the other currency is priceless to currency collectors."

Mr. Coats was silent for a few minutes before he spoke again.

"So, I have to pay the taxes on about $30 million in gold bullion, currency and other negotiables? What are the current tax rates?"

"Pretty high for something like that, Mr. Coats. However, since all the other things are tax-free, you can sit nice and pretty."

"Okay, if I agree to all this craziness you're proposing, who stole the money in the first place and where is it now?"

"The money was stolen by the bank manager. I believe, if you do a credit check or asset search on the relatives and friends of Mr. Davids, you're probably going to find someone who is deeply in debt."

"What proof do you have of this crazy scheme?"

"Simple, when you find the coffee maker and coffee pots from the bank manager's office, you will find the money. I'll even provide you with the serial numbers of those stolen bills."

"So what do you get out of all of this?"

"My client's freedom and a fresh start in life for herself and her boys."

"I still don't trust you; I want legal paperwork drawn up."

"I totally agree. Have your insurance company's attorneys draw whatever legal documents you want. Send them to me and I will notarize them in your presence along with my client and Mr. Edgeworth."

"How do I know you will keep your end of the deal after I ask for the charges to be dropped?"

"That's easy; when you drop the charges against my client and I receive a phone call from Linda about it, I'll keep my promise to you, giving you the serial numbers of the stolen bills."

"And you will provide me with other tips to this alleged treasure?"

"That's right, Mr. Coats."

Mr. Coats thought about it for almost thirty minutes before getting up and leaving Daniel's office without saying a word. Daniel did some paperwork for some other cases he had pending before locking up shop. He went home and was checking his e-mail when his home phone rang. He looked at the number that was calling him; it was Jessica.

"Hello, Jessica, what do you have for me?" asked Daniel.

"Daniel, I found out that the vault manufacturer is still in business. They changed names in 1943 to the Lake Erie Steel Company."

"Did you get the combination?"

"Yes, but that vault also requires a skeleton key to open it."

"Bring that information to the office tomorrow. I want the combination sealed inside of an envelope with your initials on the outside."

"Will do; I also found something very interesting about all those insurance companies."

"What did you find out?"

"Until Bowker & Bowker, LLC took over, the other insurance companies had one major shareholder whose last name was Busey."

"Stay on it, girl, you're on the right track and I'll see you tomorrow at the office; goodbye."

CHAPTER 14

Jessica met Daniel at the office and handed him her report along with the sealed envelope. Daniel put the envelope inside of the safe in the basement of the office. Jessica was leaving as the newspaper delivery person was walking up the steps. They stepped into the outer office with a large bundle of newspapers; Lynn looked up at them.

"Can I help you?" she asked.

"Yes, these reprinted newspapers are for Daniel Marcos," they said.

"Go ahead on into the office."

The person walked into Daniel's inner office and set the newspapers down on his desktop; Daniel looked up at them.

"How much do I owe you?"

"Nothing, Mr. Marcos, these were pre-paid for by a Jessica Kim," they replied as they left the office.

Daniel read over Jessica's report and called Bill at the bank. Daniel put Bill on speakerphone so he could ask him some questions. Lynn was sitting quietly in Daniel's office with a pen and notepad. Bill had to put Daniel on hold to take care of some business before returning to Daniel.

"Sorry to have kept you on hold for so long, what can I do for you?"

"I have some more questions for you. Would you mind if Lynn takes notes?" asked Daniel as he looked over Jessica's report one last time.

"No, go ahead and fire away, Mr. Marcos."

"Who is Jack Busey III?"

"That would be my late wife's father."

"Who is John Busey II?"

"That would have been my late wife's grandfather."

"Do you have a set of skeleton keys in your possession?"

"Yes, they are hanging up on my office wall in a display case."

"Do you know if they go to the original vault or not?"

"Yes, they do go to the original vault, Mr. Marcos."

"Are there any other living relatives of the Busey Estate and related property that you know of?"

"Only my children, but the estate paperwork was very specific that only in the event of my death would they be able to play a role on the estate."

"I see and the property across County Road F, who owns that parcel of land?"

"I do, Mr. Marcos. It is a two acre parcel that was willed to me by Jack Busey III. He wanted his daughter and her husband to build a large mansion out there; unfortunately, he died before they could get it built."

"Is the property marked clearly?"

"Yes, the west side of the fence is marked as private property; no hunting, no fishing and no shooting. The other side of the fence is BLM land."

"And the rest of the property?"

"The north side is marked by a national forest service sign for the San Juan National Forest. The east side is marked by the city limits of Ironton and, of course, the south side is marked by the County Road."

"Where was the original bank located at, again?"

"At what is now the corner of 4th Street and Grand Avenue."

"That puts it right in front of the mayor's office."

"That's right, Mr. Marcos."

"Mr. Edgeworth, I believe that you have been an unknowing and unwilling participant in a 120 year old insurance scam committed by your late wife's family."

"Do you have proof of this scam?"

"Yes, I have most of the proof. The biggest piece of proof I lack is the vault itself."

"Is there anything else I can do for you?"

"No, that's all for right now; goodbye."

Lynn left the room to type up the answers. She returned with the transcript for Daniel's review. He looked it over and initialed that as being okay. She made copies, putting one of the copies in the case file and the other she locked up in the safe in the basement.

Melanie was sitting in an exam room with a doctor discussing her options; there weren't many.

"Mrs. Thompson, I just received the latest lab results and they are not favorable. If you carry this unborn child to term, you will more than likely die. You are at an age that is considered high risk."

"So, are you telling me I should have an abortion?"

"If that is what you want, yes. I have all the equipment and drugs to do it right here."

"I can't do it and it's not for religious reasons either. I have three kids, now, that I could have had aborted, but I didn't."

"Then I suggest you make your funeral plans now. You need to get your last will and testament done. I would also suggest a living will as well; I'll give you whatever help I can. Do you know who the father is?"

"Yes, he's a kind and loving man."

"You need to tell him so that he can help you with raising all your kids."

"I promise to let them know."

"Pick up your prescriptions on the way out; goodbye."

Mr. Coats walked into Daniel's office with all the legal paperwork. Lynn brought in her notary stamps and witnessed Daniel signing the forms. She notarized the paperwork as Mr. Coats countersigned the forms. When the paperwork was completed, Daniel had Lynn make a copy to put into Melanie's case file. As Mr. Coats went to leave, Daniel stopped him.

"Mr. Coats, I surmise you went to see Linda and tried to get the charges dropped; right?"

"Yes, I did, but I don't think she'll buy it."

"I'm prepared for that contingency. My offer to help you still stands regardless if we go to trial or not. All Linda has is circumstantial evidence."

"Thank you, Mr. Marcos. Of all the attorneys I've had to deal with, you're a totally different breed."

"That's because I'm a good lawyer. I know one of these days, I'm going to stub my toe and when I do, it will cost me dearly."

"Well, now, if you ever need a job, Bowker & Bowker, LLC is always looking for good insurance investigators," said Mr. Coats, handing Daniel his business card.

"Thank you, Mr. Coats, I just might do that someday," replied Daniel, taking the card and putting it into his business card holder as Mr. Coats left his office. Daniel waited until the outer office door shut.

"Lynn, get in here with a notepad."

"Yes, Daniel."

As Lynn was about to enter the inner office, Melanie showed up. It was apparent to Lynn that she had been crying. Melanie looked at Lynn and tried to regain her composure.

"Is Daniel available? It is urgent I speak to him."

"Sure, go on inside," replied Lynn with a smile on her face.

Melanie walked into Daniel's inner office, smiled and shook Daniel's left hand before sitting down.

"What can I do for you?" asked Daniel as he looked at the tear stains on her cheeks.

"How much does it cost to have you draw up a Last Will and Testament, a Living Will and a Trust for my boys?"

"It would take me about three hours for each one because of all the legal mumbo-jumbo I would be required to put into all those documents. But, you can do all those documents on your computer from any of several Internet sources for free."

"They're simple forms?"

"Oh, yes and like I said, they're free. Just don't forget to provide a copy of that living will to your doctor. Do you also need a Durable Medical Power of Attorney?"

"No, I don't think so. What do I need to do for the trust accounts for my boys?"

"Mr. Edgeworth can help me with that one. Since you have a notary at the bank, have them sign all the forms, make copies for your doctor and yourself of the living will. If you want me to, I can file that Last Will and Testament at the city clerk's office as well as the San Juan County clerk's office."

"Thanks, you sure made it easier than I thought it would be."

"I always make it as easy as possible for my clients. Besides, my competitor at the other end of the town would charge you $600 an hour to do what you can do for free."

"How many copies of each of those documents should I keep?"

"The Last Will and Testament, you should keep the original in a safe or a safe deposit box. The trust document should be kept with the will."

"Okay and thanks for all your help."

"Anytime; by the way, did the doctor say why or what made you so sick?"

"It was as you suspected, the stress and something called PTSD."

"Post traumatic stress disorder, well is there anything else I can do for you?"

"No, I'll be on my way; goodbye," she said as she went to leave.

"Before you leave, do you use a cash counting machine at work?"

"Yes, in the main vault. The machine is an Axtar Model 7100 S, serial number A1007591."

"Okay, thank you."

Melanie left and Lynn entered the inner office.

"Lynn, type up an affidavit for a seizure warrant. I need the cash counting machine from the main vault. The make is an Axtar Model Number 7100 S, serial number A1007591."

Okay; anything else?"

"No, get that affidavit typed up and over to Marshal Beckman. I'll call Mr. Edgeworth."

Lynn nodded as she left the inner office. Daniel immediately jumped on the phone.

"Mr. Edgeworth, I need a small favor from you for Melanie's sake."

"What is it that you need, Mr. Marcos?"

"I need the cash counting machine from your main vault."

"Which one, I have three of them in there?"

"An Axtar Model 7100 S. I will be sending Marshal Beckman to pick it up."

"I'll be ready, counselor. Is there anything else?"

"No, thank you very much," said Daniel as he hung up the phone.

Linda typed up the affidavit and brought it into Daniel for his review. He made some minor changes and when Lynn brought it back in, he signed off on it. Lynn left to get it notarized and then took the affidavit to the courthouse in Silverton to be signed. His Honor, Judge Kyle Tillman signed the seizure warrant and had it delivered to Marshal Beckman. Lynn returned to the office so they could go to lunch. When lunch was over, they returned to find Mr. Coats on their doorstep; he had been badly beaten up.

"Good Lord, Mr. Coats, what happened to you?!" asked Daniel.

"Somebody ransacked my hotel room in Silverton and I walked in on them. The fight was on and I haven't had to fight that long and hard with anyone since I was in the Marine Corps; that was fifteen years ago."

"Do you need to see a doctor?" asked Lynn.

"No."

"Lynn, go get a first aid kit and call Marshal Gills; tell her what happened. Mr. Coats, did the attacker take anything?"

"Yes, my handwritten notes and some other paperwork I had."

"Mr. Coats, I rest assure you, you're on the right track to finding the stolen money and this is a prime example of a very nervous robber/murderer/extortionist."

"How do you figure that they're a murderer?" asked Mr. Coats as Lynn started first aid on his hands, right eye and the back of his head.

"Mr. Coats, the person that attacked you and took all your notes and other paperwork has to be the same one that killed the bank manager. This person then took the coffee pot, from the dead bank manager, which contains the money my client is accused of stealing."

"You're probably right, but you could be wrong."

"I don't think so and I think you had better call Mr. Homes of the FBI. Now, let's go inside my office and wait for Marshal Gills to arrive. What are you holding in your left hand?"

"Evidence."

Daniel looked up in time to see Mary, the news reporter and photographer for the Ironton Gazette leaving the scene. Daniel went directly to his office and called the editor.

"Mr. Marcos, did I print something that was offensive to you?" he asked, nervously.

"No, but you can do me, the Silverton town marshal, the DAs office and the FBI a real big favor."

"What can I do?"

"Tonight's front-page headline needs to read INSURANCE INVESTIGATOR ASSAULTED, FBI CALLED IN TO INVESTIGATE. You can use Mary's picture she took and send her to talk to Mr. Coats in Silverton. Get that headline out on the Internet as well. Somebody saw who this person is and thinks it's not important."

"Why such an urgency on this simple assault?"

"I know three things about this person which makes them really nervous."

"What are those three things, Mr. Marcos?" he asked, preparing to take notes for a possible story.

"They are a bank robber, indirectly, an extortionist and a murderer. They have also assaulted someone they thought could identify them. I am reasonably certain that they also fled the state."

"That's an interesting story; I'll get right on it."

"Thanks," said Daniel, hanging up the phone.

"Where did Mr. Coats go?" asked Daniel looking around for him.

"Marshal Gills took him to the clinic in Silverton to stitch up the back of his head. I couldn't get it to stop bleeding."

"That's okay, Lynn, call the FBI office in Denver. I want to talk to Agent Homes right away."

A few minutes later, Agent Homes called Daniel; Lynn put him through.

"Mr. Marcos, what is going on down there?"

"Mr. Coats was assaulted earlier today. I strongly suspect whoever assaulted Mr. Coats, ransacked his hotel room and took some of his paperwork, is the same person who murdered the bank manager, extorted money from him and is trying to frame my client for the bank robbery."

"So what you're saying is this assailant is an extortionist, a murderer and an assaulter? Why call me in on this case?"

"Because this person has fled the state of Colorado and they have some or all of the cash in their possession."

"And you have proof of this claim?"

"Come down here and talk to Mr. Coats. I will surmise when you find the cash, I can connect the cash to them, to the bank manager's murder, etc."

"You have proof of this as well?"

"Yes, now come down here and talk to Mr. Coats, bring a seizure warrant to serve on me for fifty-five DVDs and your phone should start ringing off the hook tonight."

"Let me guess, you put down my phone number as a point of contact for leads; right?"

"Yes, I sure did, Mr. Homes; goodbye," said Daniel hanging up the phone. He turned to face Lynn.

"Call Jessica and tell her to keep an eye on my office tonight. Tell her to be prepared for someone with above-average fighting skills."

"Right away."

Just after nightfall, Daniel and Lynn locked up and went home. Daniel drove past Jessica on his way home. After working out, he showered and had dinner. He made some tea and started reading the newspapers that had been delivered earlier that day. The newspapers were very informative to Daniel. Melanie had just finished cleaning up the kitchen and called her kids into the kitchen.

"I have to tell you all something," Melanie said.

"Mom, are you pregnant?" asked Seth.

"Yes and I decided not to have an abortion. According to Dr. Roberts, I probably won't make it through the birth process."

"See, David, I told you mom was pregnant; I bet you Mr. Marcos is the father," said Seth, grinning ear to ear.

"Mommy, is it a boy or a girl?" asked Todd.

"I don't know and I don't want to know; I want it to be a surprise. I also don't want any of you telling Mr. Marcos he is the father unless I die."

"Mr. Marcos is such a nice guy mom, why don't you tell him? I think he would understand."

"Seth, you're so stupid! If Mr. Marcos told you to jump off of a building you would do it!" yelled David. The fight was on after that with name-calling, yelling and punches being thrown. Melanie rolled her eyes and slammed her fists down on the kitchen table to restore order.

"David and Seth, I'm ashamed of you two. You don't seem to grasp the situation. I probably won't see you graduate high school, David, or college. I probably won't see you get married or see my grandkids."

She was silent a minute before speaking again.

"Seth, I probably won't be there when you get your heart broken by your first crush. I won't see you graduate high school, college or get married and have kids," said Melanie with tears in her eyes.

"Mom, don't cry, I'm sure you'll find someone who'll love us and want us," said Seth as he started to cry.

"You can count on it," said Melanie as they all hugged and cried.

The next morning, as Melanie was going to work, she saw the Christmas wish list on the kitchen table. She opened it up and saw only a few items on the list which were mostly in Seth's writing. She put the list into her pocket as she went to work.

CHAPTER 15

Saturday morning found Mr. Homes knocking on Daniel's door. Daniel dressed and had Mr. Homes drive him to his office. They entered the office and Daniel went to the basement. Daniel returned with the boxes containing the DVDs. Agent Homes looked over the DVDs before putting them into the trunk of his unmarked police car. He came back into the office.

"So, what are on all those DVDs?" asked Agent Homes.

"The serial numbers of the stolen bills. I figured out how the money was able to be stolen from the bank without too many people noticing."

"How?"

"My guess is, when I check the cash counting machine that my client used all the time, I'm going to find that it has been altered in some manner."

"I see and you say we will find a coffee pot/coffee maker in the unknown subject's possession?"

"Yes, a Western Auto coffee maker, but it doesn't work."

"I see and where should I start looking for this unknown subject?"

"I sense the presence of a gambling debt with this. I would start looking at Las Vegas, Reno and Lake Tahoe, Nevada, or Atlantic City, New Jersey."

"Thank you very much, counselor."

Daniel walked home this time. He saw Melanie coming out of the Stevens Funeral Home and Mortuary. She quickly ran from there towards the bank. Daniel spent the rest of the weekend catching up on his e-mail since Agent Homes had brought with him Daniel's computer. He just shut off his computer when his cell phone rang.

"Daniel, it's Jessica, I found out what the old Chadd mine mined," she said.

"What did it mine?"

"Officially, hematite."

"Iron ore and fairly common around here; what else?"

"Iron pyrite and Tellurium. I found out that's how the Town of Telluride got its name and it is used in the steel industry."

"Who is the current owner of the deed to the property?"

"The Department of the Interior does now. The owner was allegedly killed in a cave-in on August 11, 1934. No body was ever found during the rescue attempt and the Mine Safety Administration's agent condemned the mine. It was sealed on August 17, 1934."

"Jessica, I think you just stumbled onto something. I want a copy of the deed, a copy of the mine's alleged map and a copy of the original street map of Ironton at that time. I want you to highlight where the bank was located at the time and I will see you in my office after you get the information."

"I suppose you want a copy of the newspaper for that time too; right?"

"Yes; goodbye."

Daniel spent the holidays with Melanie and her kids. He took Seth shopping in Grand Junction one weekend. He tried to be a friend to David, but David was not so nice about it. Melanie's youngest took to Daniel right away, like Seth had done. When the holidays were over, it was back to work for Daniel. Daniel's phone was already ringing off the hook. He looked at the phone number on the display; Linda was calling. He grabbed a notepad and went into his inner office to answer the phone.

"Hello, Linda, I hope you had a good holiday break."

"I sure did, counselor, thanks for asking. Do you have a pen and notepad handy?"

"I sure do, fire away."

"The Benson case, 12CR196, I'm dropping the charges due to lack of consistency among the witnesses and the police's statements."

"Thank you, my client will be very happy."

"The Dill case, 13CR199, you asked for a continuance to gather more evidence I believe?"

"Yes, I did."

"Judge Kyle Tillman has granted your request and will see us in his courtroom on September 1 instead of May 9."

"That would be fine."

"The Garcia case, 14CR17, I'll give your client the choice of eighteen months in jail and a $1000 fine. This fine includes court costs for pleading guilty to a class III misdemeanor. Or, conviction on the F3 felony he was arrested for; six-year sentence with two years of probation."

"I'll call my client and see what they say."

"The Stevens Funeral Home and Mortuary case, 13CR751. I'll drop the charges of reckless and careless driving if your client pleads guilty to Abuse of a Corpse, C. R. S. 18-13-101 and Spilling Load on Highways Prohibited, C.R.S. 42-4-1407. I'll go for a $2500 fine, which includes court costs, no jail time and he can keep his driving privileges."

"That's very kind of you."

"The Chad case, 14CR299, I'm going to trial with this one. The trial date is September 3 in Judge Kyle Tillman's courtroom."

"I'll let my client know."

"The Blake case, 13CR605, I'm going to drop the charges due to lack of evidence."

"Thank you."

"The Clark case, 12CR989, I'm going to try with this one. Court date is September 9 in Judge Kyle Tillman's courtroom; goodbye."

Daniel hung up the phone as Lynn walked into the outer office. She started a pot of coffee and turned up the heat a little. Daniel came out with the list of items that Linda had given him. He called Linda back after having talked to Mr. Garcia.

"Hello Daniel, what can I do for you?" asked Linda.

"My client, Mr. Garcia, case number 14CR17, was hoping that you could forego the jail time if he pays cash?"

"Agreed; send him to pay the court."

"Thank you," said Daniel as he hung up the phone.

Daniel walked out into the outer office for a cup of coffee; he looked over at Lynn.

"Why hasn't Mr. Stevens called me back, yet?" asked Daniel.

"Daniel, I called him. Apparently, he had to drive to Yuma, Colorado late last night to pick up an entire family."

"I'm sorry, I didn't know."

"Trust me, Daniel, if he calls, I will put him straight through to you."

Daniel went about the rest of his day. Marshal Beckman came to Daniel's office just before lunchtime with the cash counter. A little before closing time, Mr. Stevens finally called Daniel.

"Mr. Stevens, you're a very lucky person. It appears that Linda is willing to drop the felony charges against you for you pleading guilty to two misdemeanor charges," said Daniel.

"What am I supposed to plead guilty to, Mr. Marcos?"

"Abuse of a Corpse and Spilling Load on Highways Prohibited. You keep your driving privileges and you pay a $2500 fine for the court."

"I gladly accept those terms, Mr. Marcos."

"Great, I'll call Linda. Remember, this case isn't over yet."

"I know; the family's lawyer, Mr. Bett, just delivered the civil suit."

"My sincere condolences on that issue. I think I have some information that might help you win that case."

"What did you find?"

"My private investigator found something. The hearse your company owns was purchased through a GM dealer; right?"

"Yes, the car is a GM product, but the rest of the hearse is sent to an assembly plant in Virginia, I think. The company is called Custom Hearse and Ambulance, I think."

"Then, I surmise, when the hearse is completed, it is shipped to the GM dealer for inspection and dealer prep prior to you driving it off the lot, right?"

"Right."

"My private investigator found out that the manufacture of the latch on the back of your hearse is defective. Come by my office tomorrow to pick up what she found."

"Will do, Mr. Marcos; goodbye."

Daniel hung up the phone and called Linda. Linda said she accepted Mr. Stevens' guilty pleas and was looking forward to seeing him for the fine. Daniel made sure Lynn was safely in her car and out of town before he returned home. Jessica showed up at Daniel's office the next day with all sorts of maps, pictures and the newspaper articles. Lynn was using the cash counter and scratching her head.

"What's wrong, Lynn?" asked Daniel.

"I put the same two $20 bills into the cash counter. The first time it said there were three $20 bills. The second time it said that there was only one $20 bill, even though there were two in the catch tray. The third time, it counted it right."

"So, what you're telling me, there is only a one in three chance that the money I put in there would be counted correctly?"

"Yes and look at the sides of the machine. All those paperclips are from my desk," she said, pointing at all the paperclips stuck to the sides.

"Jessica, get me the plans to the Ironton Town Bank and Trust building's lightening rod system."

"Okay, can we discuss my information now?"

"Absolutely; Lynn hold all my calls unless they are from certain people and find out how often that cash counter needs to be calibrated."

"Will do."

Daniel and Jessica stepped into Daniel's inner office. Daniel looked over the deeds and newspaper clippings. The map showed all the changes made to the town and the bank. There was one of the mine tunnels that went straight through the old Busey property. The tunnel was labeled as "for waste ore/rock." Daniel was looking over all the information, trying to connect it with his client, when he saw the name of the Mine Safety Administration inspector who had condemned the mine; Gordon Coats.

"Jessica, do a background check on Mr. Kyle Coats. I have a suspicion you're going to find that Gordon Coats is related to Kyle Coats. If such is the case, then Mr. Coats must really be watched carefully."

"I understand, Daniel; goodbye," she said as she left. Daniel's phone started ringing.

"Yes, Lynn?" asked Daniel.

"I have Agent Homes on line one for you."

"I'll take it Lynn," said Daniel, pressing down the flashing button.

"Yes, Agent Homes, what can I do for you?"

"The anonymous tip you gave me is a little confusing. Some of the serial numbers are bolded in red; do you know what that means?"

"No, I don't, but my client is supposed to call me within the hour and I will ask her that; can I call you back?"

"Yes, I am at the Secret Service office in Las Vegas, Nevada."

"I will call you; goodbye."

Melanie called a few minutes later.

"Melanie what are the bold, red serial numbers you gave me?"

"Those are the serial numbers of the $50 and $100 bills that were in my drawer one day and gone the next even though I didn't issue them."

"Did you know that the cash counter you used miscounts money two out of three times?"

"Yes and it's also magnetic. That is why I always hand-counted my drawer before I left."

"Thank you; goodbye."

Daniel called the Las Vegas, Nevada Secret Service office and passed along the information. Agent Homes called Daniel back a few hours later.

"Mr. Marcos, I would like first to say I'm sorry for the way I treated you and your client's kids. However, you were right about a possible gambling debt payoff."

"Let me guess, some of those bills have shown up in Las Vegas?"

"Yes, one particular casino and bank. I have someone in custody that I am asking a lot of questions to about the money. Your theory about the missing coffee pot was right as well."

"How much money have you recovered?"

"About $10,000 so far. The bills were very tightly wrapped, so it will take some time to count it all out."

"That's great news, Agent Homes. Is this person a relative of Mr. Davids' by any chance?"

"I haven't determined that, yet, but I highly suspect so at this time."

"Well, Agent Homes, if you need any more help from me, please call, no matter what time of the day it is; goodbye."

Lynn entered Daniel's inner office after he got off the phone.

"Daniel, I found out the cash counter needs to be calibrated, cleaned and inspected at least once a year. The last time the counter was calibrated, according to the calibration sticker I found, was seventeen years ago."

"Good work; close up shop and I'll see you on Monday."

Daniel was at home less than an hour before Agent Homes had started calling.

"Mr. Marcos, I need your help. This person appears to be a third or fourth cousin of the dead bank manager. The problem is, he's denying everything and says he was never in Colorado. If he fights extradition, I may lose this one."

"Having a little bit of a hard time connecting up the evidence, aren't you?"

"Yes, Mr. Marcos, I certainly am."

"You're not going to lose this case. I think you can prove he was in Colorado more than once. I suspect he came here once to kill his uncle and take the money. He then attacked Mr. Coats in his hotel room which puts him out here a second time."

"How can I prove both?"

"I think you'll find that there are plenty of witnesses, to include video surveillance cameras at the Las Vegas Airport, Denver International Airport and possibly the Durango Airport."

"I'll check that out; what about Mr. Coats?"

"Mr. Coats gave some evidence to Marshal Gills. This evidence should match the person you have in custody."

"What if they fight extradition?"

"I can help you out there. If you charge them and they fight extradition, I suggest you call Linda Bacara at the DAs office here and tell her to bill me for the cost of the extradition."

"Thank you, Mr. Marcos; goodbye."

Monday morning brought much needed good news. Linda, after talking to Agent Homes, agreed to drop the charges against Melanie. Daniel called Melanie to tell her the good news. She was much relieved as she hung up the phone. Linda let Daniel know that the state was going to renovate the courthouse they used so Daniel was free for the summer. Daniel started making his plans for the trip with Melanie's boys to the John Martin State Wildlife Area and John Martin Reservoir.